"You Are Beautiful," Ethan Said.

She stared at him. He'd sounded utterly sincere.

"And I don't mean all the usual stuff, that you're smart, and kind, and compassionate, and that that makes you beautiful. Although it's all true. I mean beautiful in the literal sense."

Layla was having trouble breathing. She could only continue to stare at him. It wasn't that she hadn't been told all this before. But never like this, or by a man like Ethan.

"I mean it," he said. "I just realized I've been looking at women I would have found attractive once, and all I can think of is how skinny they are."

He focused on her suddenly. She felt a bit dizzy, then realized she was holding her breath. She let it out, slowly.

"Come to dinner with me," he said suddenly.

"I'll go change," she said softly.

Move over, Cinderella. 15

Dear Reader,

Spring is in the air…and so is romance. Especially at Silhouette, where we're celebrating our 20th anniversary throughout 2000! And Silhouette Desire promises you six powerful, passionate, provocative love stories *every month*.

Fabulous Anne McAllister offers an irresistible MAN OF THE MONTH with *A Cowboy's Secret*. A rugged cowboy fears his darkest secret will separate him from the beauty he loves.

Bestselling author Leanne Banks continues her exciting miniseries LONE STAR FAMILIES: THE LOGANS with a sexy bachelor doctor in *The Doctor Wore Spurs*. In *A Whole Lot of Love,* Justine Davis tells the emotional story of a full-figured woman feeling worthy of love for the first time.

Kathryn Jensen returns to Desire with another wonderful fairy-tale romance, *The Earl Takes a Bride*. THE BABY BANK, a brand-new theme promotion in Desire in which love is found through sperm bank babies, debuts with *The Pregnant Virgin* by Anne Eames. And be sure to enjoy another BRIDAL BID story, which continues with Carol Devine's *Marriage for Sale,* in which the hero "buys" the heroine at auction.

We hope you plan to usher in the spring season with all six of these supersensual romances, only from Silhouette Desire!

Enjoy!

Joan Marlow Golan

Joan Marlow Golan
Senior Editor, Silhouette Desire

Please address questions and book requests to:
Silhouette Reader Service
U.S.: 3010 Walden Ave., P.O. Box 1325, Buffalo, NY 14269
Canadian: P.O. Box 609, Fort Erie, Ont. L2A 5X3

A Whole Lot of Love

JUSTINE DAVIS

Published by Silhouette Books

America's Publisher of Contemporary Romance

This is for all the big girls
who have felt the sting of careless cruelty.

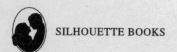 SILHOUETTE BOOKS

ISBN 0-373-76281-X

A WHOLE LOT OF LOVE

Copyright © 2000 by Janice Davis Smith

This edition published by arrangement with Harlequin Books S.A.

® and TM are trademarks of Harlequin Books S.A., used under license. Trademarks indicated with ® are registered in the United States Patent and Trademark Office, the Canadian Trade Marks Office and in other countries.

Visit us at www.romance.net

Printed in U.S.A.

JUSTINE DAVIS

lives in San Clemente, California. Her interests outside of writing are sailing, doing needlework, horseback riding and driving her restored 1967 Corvette roadster—top down, of course.

A policewoman, Justine says that years ago, a young man she worked with encouraged her to try for a promotion to a position that was, at that time, occupied only by men. "I succeeded, became wrapped up in my new job, and that man moved away, never, I thought, to be heard from again. Ten years later he appeared out of the woods of Washington State, saying he'd never forgotten me and would I please marry him. With that history, how could I write anything but romance?"

IT'S OUR 20th ANNIVERSARY!
We'll be celebrating all year, continuing with these fabulous titles, on sale in March 2000.

Special Edition

 #1309 Dylan and the Baby Doctor
Sherryl Woods

#1310 Found: His Perfect Wife
Marie Ferrarella

 #1311 Cowboy's Caress
Victoria Pade

 #1312 Millionaire's Instant Baby
Allison Leigh

 #1313 The Marriage Promise
Sharon De Vita

#1314 Good Morning, Stranger
Laurie Campbell

Intimate Moments

 #991 Get Lucky
Suzanne Brockmann

 #992 A Ranching Man
Linda Turner

 #993 Just a Wedding Away
Monica McLean

 #994 Accidental Father
Lauren Nichols

#995 Saving Grace
RaeAnne Thayne

#996 The Long Hot Summer
Wendy Rosnau

Romance

 #1432 A Royal Masquerade
Arlene James

 #1433 Oh, Babies!
Susan Meier

#1434 Just the Man She Needed
Karen Rose Smith

#1435 The Baby Magnet
Terry Essig

 #1436 Callie, Get Your Groom
Julianna Morris

#1437 What the Cowboy Prescribes...
Mary Starleigh

Desire

 #1279 A Cowboy's Secret
Anne McAllister

 #1280 The Doctor Wore Spurs
Leanne Banks

#1281 A Whole Lot of Love
Justine Davis

#1282 The Earl Takes a Bride
Kathryn Jensen

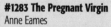 **#1283 The Pregnant Virgin**
Anne Eames

 #1284 Marriage for Sale
Carol Devine

One

"**Y**ou wouldn't be averse to selling your body for a good cause, would you?"

Ethan Winslow's first thought was that this woman had the sexiest voice he'd ever heard. His second was that if he didn't pay attention, he would end up following that low, husky, seductive, downright erotic voice into who knew what kind of mess.

"Look, Ms...."

"Laraway."

"Ms. Laraway, I appreciate your effort, but I'd just as soon write a check."

She laughed. Damn, the laugh was even sexier, deep and sensual. "We'll gladly take that, too. But we'd really like something more...corporeal, as well."

"My backside on the block?" he asked wryly.

"I've heard it's a fine backside."

She said it so cheerfully that he found himself grinning in spite of himself. He was sitting here casually discussing his backside, and the auctioning off of same, with a woman he'd never met but who had the kind of voice that gave men X-rated dreams.

"And who told you that?"

"Oh, you have many fans in town, Mr. Winslow."

Are you one of them? he wondered almost hopefully. If she looked anything like her voice, he might reconsider doing something about his dismal social life.

"Surely you wouldn't want to disappoint them?" the voice said. "You could bring in the largest donation of the night, from what I've been told."

"You've been told," he said, "way too much."

"It's a character flaw," she said with a dramatic sigh. "People talk to me."

Ethan laughed. It felt odd, and he wondered if his baby sister was right and he really had become too darn serious. He leaned back in his chair, turning his head slightly to avoid being toasted by the southern California sun pouring through his office window.

"I can see why," he said.

"They also find it very hard to say no to me."

He didn't doubt it; he wondered if there was a man on earth who could listen to this voice for long and still say no. To whatever she asked. He wondered idly if she'd found her way into this work because she knew the effect it had, that voice. Maybe she'd learned somewhere along the way that she could use it to loosen the wallet of any male.

At least she'd chosen to use it in a good way, if that were the case, he thought.

"You see," she went on, "I'm very...persistent."

"So are bill collectors."

She laughed, that wonderful laugh again. "Some people see it that way, I know. But I prefer to think of it more like a puppy begging at the table, with big sad eyes that you try to ignore but can't. Then you end up feeling guilty and give them what they want."

He chuckled. "So, you admit you use guilt?"

"Absolutely," she answered blithely. "It's one of my best tools. Besides, once people give, they feel so much better."

His chuckle became another laugh. "So it's for their own good, then?"

"Absolutely. And ours, of course, but you see, that's the best part. Everyone winds up happier. So, may I add you to the roster?"

It was on the tip of his tongue to say yes. His mouth was open to say yes. Then, at the last second, he remembered what he would be saying yes to. He'd never been to one of those kinds of charity auctions before, but visions of beauty pageant contestants were vivid in his mind.

Uh-uh. No way.

Lord, she'd almost had him, with her cheerful demeanor, her sense of humor…and that voice.

Almost.

"Listen, Ms. Laraway, I have a meeting scheduled in ten minutes. I'll consider your…request, but I have to go."

"Certainly. My goal is to convince you to volunteer, certainly not to interfere with your work," the sexy voice said, and he wondered again why he didn't just say yes. "But please, do think about it. I'll get back to you."

He did think about it. In fact, when his assistant stuck her head in the door and reminded him that his meeting was to begin in approximately forty-five seconds, and that the staff was already in the adjacent meeting room, he realized he'd been thinking about it for the entire ten minutes.

Or rather, thinking about the amusing, sexy-voiced Ms. Laraway. He wasn't going to participate in her auction—parading himself around like a horse in a sale ring wasn't his idea of fun—but it was tempting, if only to meet the woman.

He gathered the papers he'd been going over in preparation for the meeting before he'd been interrupted by the call. He started toward the meeting room door, but stopped as his assistant turned to go back out to her desk.

"Karen?"

She turned, looking at him questioningly. He'd inherited both Karen Yamato and this office when Pete Collins had turned over the reins to him and retired. His old mentor had told him that Karen was both the glue that held things together and the oil that kept them running, and it hadn't taken Ethan long to realize Pete had been understating things a bit. The petite, ageless-seeming Eurasian woman, who looked to him exactly as she had when he'd first come here as a boy, was as close as anybody around West Coast Technologies came to being indispensable. And that included him.

"Did you get a number from the woman who just called? From the Alzheimer's charity?"

"Layla? Of course."

Layla? Her name was Layla? A voice like that, and a name like Layla Laraway? The mind fairly boggled, he thought. And his own mind was conjuring up all kinds of heated, sweaty images.

"Did you change your mind and decide to do the auction?"

"I…no. I just wanted to know when it was. I forgot to ask." *I need to know how much time I have to come up with an excuse.* Then he frowned. "How did you know I wasn't going to do it?"

Karen lifted a brow at him, reminding him without a word that even after only five years, she knew him almost as well as she'd known Pete after twenty years of working for him. Perhaps it was in part because he'd learned so much from her former boss that he'd taken on some of his characteristics. He didn't mind; he could do a hell of a lot worse than emulate Pete Collins. Or, at least, the Pete who had sat in this office.

He fought off the old pang and was glad when Karen offered a distraction.

"I'll call Layla back for you during your meeting, if you'd like," she said.

He looked at her, curious about the familiarity in her tone. "You know her?"

"Only by reputation."

"Which is?"

"Smart. Dynamic. Dedicated." Three things guaranteed to gain Karen's approval, Ethan thought. "What I've heard, I admire," she added.

He knew too well that no one won Karen Yamato's admiration lightly; if Layla Laraway—Lord, what a name—had gotten it without even a face-to-face, she had to be something.

"So you think I should do it?"

"I think," she said, with a gesture toward the door, "you should go to your meeting."

He jerked upright; he'd actually forgotten. Again.

He was still shaking his head as he walked into the room. He was rarely so scattered. He didn't want to think a single phone call from an unknown woman had done it, because that would mean he would have to consider that both his sisters were right about his dearth of a social life, and that he was rapidly losing what they called his minimal social skills.

"We understood that you needed at least a year after you broke up with Gwen," Margaret had told him just yesterday. "You were together a long time. But now it's been three years. It's time."

"What is it with women?" he'd asked, figuring the best defense was a diversion. "Do you always put time limits on things like that?"

"Only," his oldest sister had returned dryly, "when our brother is turning into a workaholic monk."

"You're too damn sexy to be celibate," Sarah had put in.

Now *that* had scattered him. She was his baby sister, for crying out loud, she wasn't supposed to be thinking things like that, let alone saying them.

Of course, she was twenty-eight now. He supposed she

wasn't quite the innocent he'd held in the dark the night their world had fallen apart. But still, it was hard not to think of her as that frightened ten-year-old sometimes. He—

"Ethan? Are you ready to start?"

He, Ethan thought as he snapped back to the present, was losing it. Definitely.

He glanced at his head of Research and Development, Mark Ayala, whose report on the progress on the Collins project was the reason for this meeting. He knew what he would hear, which was no change in the status quo, but he would take that happily over any setbacks. He'd only begun the project ten months ago, expected it to take years, and considered it worth the time and expense.

"Sorry, Mark," he said as he took his seat at the head of the long table. "Let's get to it."

Mark began, in that report-making drone that always reminded Ethan of Professor Kosell's economic theory classes. He'd always sat in the back of the theater-style lecture hall, high up and close to the door, so he could escape quickly and make it to work in the scant fifteen minutes he'd had to get across town. Unfortunately, the back part of the room was also the highest part of the room, where the heat of a hundred or so bodies rose, and that, coupled with his usual lack of sleep and the professor's monotone, had frequently been enough to have him nodding off.

Ethan didn't care for these types of meetings. He'd found most people too intimidated by the formal setting to really cut loose with any original thinking. He much preferred to keep current on projects by visiting his people in their own environment, where the actual work was being done. And for original thinking, he was much more likely to take a group out for pizza and beer, and let the ideas flow.

He liked the fact that West Coast Technologies was still small enough to do that, and he planned on keeping it that way. Pete had been a firm believer in "If it ain't broke..." and Ethan was content to hold that line for now. He knew they couldn't compete with all the large companies around, so he focused on specializing, working on things that had the potential to be multifunctional, or highly useful to a smaller group of people.

And then there were his pet projects, such as this one. Ethan made himself tune back in, as he sensed from Mark's tone that he was finally winding down.

"—can see, overall, things look very promising. The difference between the control group and the ones with the implant are marked."

"How much longer are your tests scheduled to run?" Ethan asked.

Mark leaned back in his chair, scratched a bit at his beard, then said, "Another two months before we move on to the next phase." He looked down at his notes, then back at Ethan. "Speaking of that, it would be so much more helpful if we could—"

Ethan held up his hand, knowing what was coming. "Sorry. There's got to be a better way to test this than to perform a dozen mouse lobotomies. That should be our last resort. I don't like the idea of intentionally and permanently destroying their memory just to see if we can fix it."

"They're *mice,*" Mark said. "And pampered ones at that. The best food, comfy cages with fresh shavings every day...my dog doesn't live as well as these guys do."

"Maybe you should take better care of your dog," Ethan said, but jokingly. "Think of another way, Mark. I know you can. Maybe...something temporary?"

The R and D head looked at him, then sighed. "I'll try. I'm checking on a chemical that supposedly temporarily affects that part of the brain, but I'm not sure how it might affect results for our purposes." He shrugged. "Maybe I should just get 'em drunk."

Ethan grinned. "Ouch. Crabby, hungover mice. But better than psychotic ones." He glanced down the table at Moira

O'Donnell, the production manager. "You're current, Moira?"

The redhead nodded. She tapped at her notepad with a long, flame-red nail. "I've tracked the necessary changes as we go. We can go into production within seven days and have enough on the market to give us a nice head start on any deconstruction copy-catters."

Ethan understood her concern. With any such product, no matter how complex, you had to expect that as soon as a competitor could get his or her hands on it—legitimately or otherwise—they would be taking it apart to study its construction, then building their own. Every amount of inventory you could get on the market before that happened solidified your hold on the market. Even if it was years away, they needed to be ready.

But in Ethan's mind, that didn't apply here. "Thanks, Moira. But on this one, put your focus on speed, not foiling industrial espionage. If we succeed, I'm not looking to make a fortune, I just want it available to as many people as possible as soon as possible."

Moira nodded, although she didn't look happy. It was her competitive nature, Ethan guessed. But that nature was part of what made her so good at her job, and on most other projects it paid off.

He shifted his gaze to the representative from the W.C.T. legal department. "So, how goes the war on your end, David?"

"The FDA," David Grayfox said with a grimace, "is the biggest pain in the—"

Again Ethan held up a hand. "Yeah, I know. So we can expect approval for voluntary human testing in about two zillion twenty-five?"

"About," David mumbled.

"Keep pushing. We have to determine if what works on our pampered, well-fed and wonderfully housed lab mice will work as well on the human brain."

He knew he was stating the obvious; this was, after all, the entire point of the Collins project.

"Yeah," Mark added offhandedly as he gathered his papers, "we may all need it someday."

Ethan knew Mark hadn't meant it that way, but nevertheless, the joking rejoinder dug deep into a sore spot that had never healed.

"Pray that you don't," he said, unable to stop the edge that came into his voice.

Mark looked at him, startled, then sheepish, as if he only now realized what he'd said. "Right, boss," he muttered, and Ethan knew that, from the generally anarchistic Mark, the title "boss" was tantamount to an apology.

Ethan nodded and stood, indicating the meeting was over. The others exited the room, and he started back toward his office. Karen caught his eye; she already had the receiver to her ear, but gestured at the phone on her desk, and he saw that two lines were lit. She mouthed a name at him.

Layla.

To his amazement, since he had a perfectly reasonable question to ask her, he hesitated. He stood there, staring down at the lit phone line as if it had the power to shock him if he touched it.

Only when he realized Karen was looking at him rather oddly did he nod and stride past her into his office. He stood behind his desk, looking down at his own phone, where the second line blinked tauntingly. He set down his notepad. Then his pen. Then himself, noticing that the creak of his leather desk chair seemed louder than usual.

Odd, how he had no trouble saying no in a business framework, but when it came to things like this, especially for charity, it was much more difficult. He had so little time, he'd made it a habit to say no to everything that required more than a monetary donation, and even those he picked rather carefully.

So he would say no again. Simple.

He stared at the phone.

He shouldn't keep her waiting. He'd in essence called her, after all.

He would just tell her no. He couldn't—wouldn't—do it.

He cleared his throat and picked up the phone.

"How was your meeting?" were her first words after he said hello. "Constructive?"

Somewhat relieved at the subject, he answered, "More a case of not regressing. Not much progress, but no bad news."

"Sometimes that's good news."

He found himself smiling. "Yes, sometimes it is."

"There's a lot to be said for no forward progress, if it also means not sliding back to the bottom of the mountain."

It was so close to his own thoughts that he couldn't help chuckling. "Exactly."

"It wasn't by chance about the memory chip, was it?"

His amusement vanished in a rush. The Collins project wasn't hush-hush, but it wasn't general knowledge, either. Certainly not outside the industry.

She seemed to understand his sudden silence. "It's why you were added to my list since last year, Mr. Winslow. We're loosely affiliated with the national Alzheimer's Association, and they track people who are doing research in the arena, even privately."

"Oh." He relaxed; they had had contact with several of the leading research facilities, any of which could have mentioned the project. And it wasn't as if she shouldn't know, given her connection. "Sorry. Reflex."

"One you've had to develop, I imagine. It must be frustrating to put a lot of time and money into something, only to have someone else beat you to it."

"It is. But in this case, I'd celebrate, if theirs worked. As long as it gets done."

"That's…an admirable attitude."

Ethan felt suddenly uncomfortable. He'd had his share—more than his share, he thought—of nominations for sainthood, and he didn't like it. Or maybe he just didn't like it that the world had become a place where what he did, which was only what he thought had to be done, made him so different in the eyes of many.

"As is what you're doing," she added. "If your chip should work, it could become instrumental in the treatment of Alzheimer's."

"'If,'" he said dryly, "is a very big word. Especially in this case."

"Trying to jog the human memory bank is tricky, computer chip or not." He could almost hear her smiling as she added, "And some mornings are harder than others."

Since he seemed to be having one of those mornings, he couldn't help but laugh. Damn, but she was going to be hard to say no to. But he was still going to do it.

"Look, about your auction—"

"When I asked you to think about it," she put in, sounding amused, "I did mean for more than an hour."

It did, now that she mentioned it, seem a bit churlish to turn her down after that short a time. His "No" died unspoken. "I...just needed to know when it is."

"Ah. To see how much time you have to wiggle out of volunteering."

Embarrassed that she'd called it so accurately, he said, "No."

"Oh?"

"To see how much time I have to wiggle out of it gracefully."

She laughed. He'd been right, it was a wonderful sound, full and rich in that low, sexy voice. "It's much easier to simply give in gracefully, Mr. Winslow."

This was odd, he thought. He'd been in high-pressure business negotiations where he hadn't felt the least bit persuaded by any power tactics, yet he was feeling it here.

"And you don't have to come up with your 'Evening to

Remember' plans right now. I only need them a week ahead, so you have a few days.''

Ah, he thought, at last, the answer to his question. ''So, it's the weekend after next?''

''Yes, on Saturday evening. There are no real rules for the evening you plan, it can be fun or elegant or creative, so you can keep it safely impersonal. If you need any help, feel free to call. I always have suggestions.''

After her promise to call him back and her cheerful good-bye, he hung up and sat looking at his phone. The sound of her voice echoed in his mind, along with the sound of his own laughter. He didn't know how much time had passed before he remembered.

He never had told her no.

He had the oddest feeling he'd just been flattened by a velvet steamroller.

Two

"**D**arlin', for you, anything. Will you be there?"

Layla smothered a sigh. "I'm the event coordinator, so, yes, I'll be there. I'll be busy all evening."

"But not all night, I hope." If ever a man could leer over the phone, it was this one.

"I'll put you down, then, Mr. Humbert. I'll need your plan for your auction date by next Friday. And thank you."

She hung up gratefully.

She pushed back an errant strand of blond hair, propped her elbows on her desk and let her head rest in her hands. Just for a moment, she thought. It couldn't hurt.

It was always this way, she told herself, right before the annual fund-raiser. Crazy, endless and exhausting. No reason to feel any more tired than usual at this time of year. But she did.

It was Humbert and his lack of subtlety. It shouldn't have gotten to her—she'd heard much worse before—but somehow this time it had been more wearing. Maybe the effect of all this verbal leering was cumulative. Or maybe she was just tired of hearing it, knowing how the tone would change when they saw her.

She knew why it happened. It had been the bane of her existence since she'd been old enough to notice. A name like Layla Laraway and a voice people likened to classic Lauren Bacall, and she was doomed. The combination of voice and name had been more curse than blessing. At least for her. For someone else, it might have been a boon. For someone else, someone the name and voice would fit.

"How'd it go?"

Layla leaned back and looked at her boss, who was standing in the doorway of her small office. "Mr. Humbert agreed to participate."

"Layla, you are a wonder!" Harry Chandler shook his head. "You could get a freezing man to give you his last piece of firewood."

"Now there's a charming visual," she said dryly.

"I never said you *would,* just that you *could.* You turn that voice on a guy and he's helpless. Nice work."

She knew that to some extent it was true, but it wasn't something she was necessarily proud of. True, it produced well for her chosen work, and she wasn't ashamed of using it for that purpose. But she knew that this was the only way she could justify it; anything less than a cause like this one would make what she could do distasteful.

"So, are we all set with the auction lineup?"

"Almost. Martina Jennings said yes, and Gloria Van Alden hasn't called me back yet, but she gave a fairly definite yes earlier."

"She'll do it," Harry said. "She loves getting up there in her finest diamonds and offering a package no one else can afford."

"Yes," Layla agreed, "but she bids as well, and generously."

"Amen," Harry said. "How about the men?"

"One holdout. Ethan Winslow."

Harry's brows furrowed. "Don't know the name. Is he new?"

She nodded. "Since last year. He runs West Coast Technologies. He popped up on the list after the compilers discovered they were starting a research project on a computer chip that could be used to jump-start the memory center of the brain in Alzheimer's patients."

Harry's brows went up. "I remember reading about that. It'd be a miracle, if they can do it."

She nodded again. She'd been impressed by the information she'd read. Ethan Winslow had begun his project quietly, without fanfare, but with a determination to see it through. It could take years, but he'd said in the one brief interview he'd done that he was prepared for that. But what had impressed her more—and had made her make the call—was the mention at the end of the article that it appeared this was Winslow's personal baby, and that he was providing a sizable part of the funding out of his own pocket. The reporter had dug a little deeper, learning from someone on staff that Winslow's feeling was that since he and W.C.T. could afford to fund it, they did so, leaving grant money from the Alzheimer's Association to go to other researchers who might not have his resources.

"Sounds like our kind of people. Do you think he'll do it?"

"I don't know. I'm going to call him back tomorrow." And, surprisingly, she was looking forward to it. She'd enjoyed talking with him, bantering, hearing him laugh. Talk about sexy voices, she thought. Ethan Winslow had the kind of voice women saved on their answering machines, just so they could hear it again. The kind of voice that could read the phone book and set your pulse racing. The kind of voice that made lonely nights seem longer. And hotter. The kind of voice—

"You'll reel him in, girl," Harry said, derailing her rather reckless train of thought. "You always do."

He went back to his own office—not much bigger than hers—leaving her pondering his last words.

"Dedicated, smart, dynamic…sounds like somebody trying to sell you on a blind date who's a dog." Bill Stanley laughed at his own joke as he and Ethan inspected the new skis Bill was considering.

Ethan grimaced wryly; it was true, if unkind. But then, Bill had never been the soul of sensitivity, even as a boy.

"If you heard her voice, you wouldn't be saying that."

His old friend's brows rose. "She gives good phone, huh?"

"If you want to put it that way," Ethan said, his tone wry, because Bill was more accurate than not. He wouldn't have worded it quite like that, but remembering his reaction to her voice, he couldn't deny there was some truth in it.

"Well, whatever she looks like, she's a step up from your current state."

He couldn't deny that, either. Lying awake last night, he'd found himself trying to remember exactly when his last real date—meaning something not connected to his work—had been.

He couldn't remember.

"Too expensive," Bill said, putting down the ski he'd been hefting. "I think I can get a deal from a guy I know."

Ethan shrugged; Bill could always get a deal from somebody. They went through this every time he wanted something; Bill would go pick a salesperson's brain, Ethan's brain—not that he knew much about skiing—anybody's brain, then go buy it someplace else.

"So," Bill said as they abandoned the search, "are you going to put yourself on the block, flaunt yourself for sex-starved society matrons to make bids on your studly body?"

"It's a charity auction, Bill. Not a sex-slave auction."

"Too bad," Bill quipped. Then, finally, he turned serious. "Are you going to do it? Hey, I'd even buy a ticket to see that!"

Ethan grimaced. "I'll give her your name, you can take my place."

As soon as he said it, Ethan regretted the words. He didn't want to think about Layla Laraway turning that voice loose on Bill.

"Hey, if she turns out to be as sexy as you say, why not?"

"Very charitable of you," Ethan said pointedly as they exited the sporting goods store. Bill got the message and became serious.

"Okay, buddy, kidding aside, I know you care about the cause."

"A lot of people care about the cause."

"But you especially care, because of Pete."

Ethan's jaw tightened. He fought down the silly notion that had been floating around in his mind for the past twenty-four hours, that somehow, if he did this, went so public with his support, it would put the seal on Pete's fate, make it impossible to deny.

Bill left it until they were seated in his car. "How is he? Have you seen him lately?"

Ethan didn't want to talk about it. Didn't want to remember. Ironic, he thought. But Bill was waiting, looking at him curiously, and he forced the words out.

"Last time I was there, he didn't know me."

He didn't mention how long ago it had been. He wasn't proud of how he'd cut and run, but he simply hadn't been able to make himself go back.

"That's rough," Bill said in that sympathetic tone Ethan had learned to despise from anyone, a sympathy offered without any real understanding. He knew Bill genuinely felt bad for him; they'd been friends for nearly all their lives, since their families had moved to the same block. Although Bill was a year older, they'd gone to all the same schools. Bill was one of the few things in Ethan's life that hadn't changed, and he valued the relationship because of it. But Bill's life had been blissfully devoid of misfortune, so he didn't really understand.

"I know how much he meant to you," Bill said.

"He's not dead yet," Ethan snapped, irked at Bill's use of the past tense.

Bill pulled back. "Touchy today, aren't you? I swear, you need to get yourself la—"

Ethan held up a hand before Bill could finish his prescription for his sex life. "If that was the answer to everything, the way you think it is, you'd be a full partner by now."

He knew that would sufficiently distract Bill; his lack of progress in the law firm he worked for was enough to start him on a diatribe that would go on as long as his listener could stand it.

Ethan put on an expression of attentiveness, but he'd heard it all before, given Bill his opinion before, and didn't see any point in doing it again when he knew his friend wouldn't make a move until he was ready. So instead he sat silently, letting Bill run on, while his mind went…elsewhere.

By the time Bill dropped him off at home, Ethan had admitted to himself that he was quite looking forward to his next call from the persuasive Ms. Laraway. Even if he was still determined to say no.

"Do you do the auction itself?" Ethan asked.

He sounded merely curious, so Layla tamped down any suspicions that he might have a motive for asking. From the beginning, many of the men she called started asking questions about her part in the proceedings. It had taken Harry—gentle, tactful Harry—to explain to her that they wanted to be sure they got a look at her, after hearing her voice. He'd left it at that, but Layla knew perfectly well that he knew what generally happened after that. She'd been doing this for six years now, and some things never changed.

"No, we hire a pro to run the actual auction. Adds momentum."

"I'll bet."

"Now, for your date, I highly recommend that you make it something you enjoy doing anyway. Makes the evening easier to get through if you for some reason don't hit it off with your companion."

"Does that happen a lot?"

"No, most people have a great time. You already have something in common with your date, caring about Alzheimer's research. There's something very feel-good about doing it, I think. And having no romantic expectations helps everyone relax."

"So, no matches made in heaven have come out of this?" he said wryly.

"Actually, a couple of relationships have grown out of it, but we haven't had a wedding yet."

"You'd have to be the maid of honor," Ethan said. "Or matron."

Layla's tapping of her pencil on her notepad—a habit she'd never had until talking to this man—stopped. Was this some subtle probe to see if she was married?

Of course not, she told herself.

And this kind of silly speculation was unlike her. She made herself focus and leave the foolishness behind.

"Afraid I don't do weddings, this auction is more than enough," she said, purposely but cheerfully misunderstanding his intent. "Now, back to your arrangements."

"What if it's something you like, but your...companion hates?" he asked, seeming to let her change the subject easily enough.

"Then hopefully she won't bid on you," Layla said with a laugh; she was delighted that he still hadn't said no. Each minute that she could keep that from happening upped the likelihood that it wouldn't. And, she admitted, allowed her to keep talking to him. "Although I can't vouch for the sanity of some women in the heat of bidding on an attractive man. Of course, we encourage that. It *is* all for a good cause, after all.''

"I appreciate your efforts and enthusiasm, Ms. Laraway, but I'm afraid most of your bidders would find what I'd come up with rather boring."

He wanted to say no. He intended to say no. She sensed that. And she wasn't sure why he hadn't yet.

"You might be surprised," she said. "Some people prefer...simpler things."

"Like you? What's your idea of the ideal evening?"

Listening to you talk. Then she sat up sharply, realizing with a little shock what she'd just thought. For the first time in her life she had an inkling of what the men she talked to were feeling. Quickly she pulled herself back together and went for the diversion.

"Sorry, I can't bid. Conflict of interest and all." As if she ever would, anyway... "Why don't I send you a list of the ones I already have, so you can get an idea of what's being offered, and you can go from there?"

He didn't respond for a moment, and with an instinct honed fine in six years of this work, she knew he had reached the moment of decision. And that same instinct—augmented by a gut-level feeling she didn't question—told her the time for ignoring his objections and reservations was gone. Told her that this was a man who would prefer honesty and forthrightness.

"Mr. Winslow, if you've seriously considered this and are still uncomfortable with it—in other words, if the benefit you see doesn't outweigh your hesitation—just tell me and I'll remove you from the list, and you won't hear from me again."

Again there was a brief silence. Then suddenly, unexpectedly, "I'll do it."

This time it was she who hesitated. Odd, she thought; she

was usually eager to jump in and cement the concession. "You're sure?" she asked instead.

"I said I'll do it." He sounded the tiniest bit cranky, as if now that he'd made the decision, he didn't want it questioned. "Send me that info you mentioned."

"I will. Right away." And then, recovering her inexplicably shaken poise, she added, "Thank you, Mr. Winslow."

"If I'm going to sacrifice my body for the cause," he said dryly, "the least you can do is call me Ethan."

"All right. Ethan."

It felt strange to even say. And not until she had did she realize she'd been avoiding using his first name even in her thoughts, despite the easy familiarity they'd achieved in their phone calls.

She managed a polite goodbye, hung up, picked up her pen and added Ethan Winslow's name to her list.

And wondered where her usual sense of accomplishment was.

Layla made a last-minute check in the mirror. Her long black dress was the best she had, the small but lovely diamond necklace and earrings her father had given to her sparkled, her makeup was perfect and her hair was tidily tucked into its French twist. Nothing could change the basics she had to work with, but she'd dressed up the dandelion as best she could.

She wanted to be out there at the door of the hotel ballroom, to thank the people who had volunteered to help. It was also best if she got the first contact with those who were new to the auction out of the way early. After that, it would be easier on her if she simply kept out of sight until it was her time to go on stage—Lord, she hated stepping out into that spotlight—but she felt she owed at least a personal thank-you to those who were giving of their time and subjecting themselves to the good-natured revelry of the auction.

She had already met most of the people who would be

coming, but there were three she had not. The woman she hadn't met was the head of a small local chain of specialty coffee shops; she had laughed and said yes almost immediately. The two men had required further convincing, although Harry, as always, joked that they just wanted her to call them back so they could listen to her voice again. She'd always laughed, shaking her head at the idea.

After talking to Ethan Winslow, she wasn't laughing anymore.

If she were honest, she would admit that meeting him was what had her on edge. Which was the last thing she needed tonight, when it was up to her to see that things went smoothly. It was unlike her, too; she had long passed the point of letting such things bother her.

Resolutely, she made her way to the door to join Harry in the greetings. The first few people she knew, and by the time she had greeted them and chatted for a moment, she was back in the groove and relaxing. Gloria Van Alden made her smile; the woman might be sixty-two, but she outshone many of the more practiced young glamour girls with her poise and class. She'd led a fascinating life, traveling around the world until her husband fell prey to the killer they were stalking tonight.

If I were a man, I'd bid on her in a second just to hear the stories she could tell, Layla thought. In fact, she added to herself with an inward grin, she would like to bid on her anyway, and she would be willing to bet Gloria would understand perfectly. Gloria knew she was fascinating. Sometimes Layla longed for that kind of bone-deep confidence.

She was still smiling after the woman when she heard Harry's voice, "Layla? You haven't met Mr. Winslow yet, have you?"

She took a quick breath and held it. She knew what was coming. She'd seen it so often before, she was past being hurt by it. If she'd been scarred, deformed or even missing some visible parts, the reaction would have been little different. But she was none of those things. Her sin was much greater; she was, quite simply, a big woman. She'd left single-digit sizes behind at age twelve and had never been back. She'd grown used to comments like "You have such a lovely face" or "Your hair is so gorgeous," the subtext unmistakably being "You'd be beautiful if you'd just lose some weight."

At twenty-three she had determinedly starved herself to the point of passable thinness—and had spent her twenty-fifth birthday in the hospital. On that day she'd had an epiphany of sorts. Just as, at five-ten, she would never be petite, she would never be model-thin, either. She would, she decided as she lay in that hospital bed, with needles in her arm, settle for healthy and fit. It was the best she could manage, and it would have to do.

And, for the most part, it did. Her doctor was happy, she could keep pace with Harry, who was a long-distance bike rider; could match her marathon-running best friend Stephanie for at least half of her training runs; and above all she felt good.

Except at times like this.

Slowly, she turned around.

He was every bit as attractive as she'd been told. Were it not for the sharp glint of intelligence in his vivid blue eyes, he would be the walking cliché of tall, dark and handsome, she thought ruefully. Dressed in a tux that fit too exquisitely to be rented, he was...he was...

He was just as sexy as he sounded on the phone.

He stared at her, and she knew he was realizing she was not.

She told herself she hadn't winced, not even inwardly. She'd expected this, after all. She waited to hear the inevitable "You're Layla?" in a tone of disbelief, waited to see his intent expression turn to one of disappointment. Then would come the awkward pause, which varied in length depending on the mental acuity or grace of the man.

Ethan Winslow, it seemed, had a lot of both; his look of surprise vanished after a split second, and he held his hand out to her without hesitation.

"Congratulations, Ms. Laraway."

A little startled at his speed, it took her a moment to take the proffered hand. Recovering, she lifted a brow at him. "For getting you here?"

He smiled. It was breathtaking. "That, too. But I meant, this looks like quite a production."

"Oh, it is," Harry said heartily. "And we couldn't pull it off without Layla. She's indispensable."

"I'm sure she is. Anybody who could talk me into this…"

Harry laughed brightly. "She *is* amazing." He turned to an attractive brunette in a silvery evening gown, one of the ushers for the evening. "Cheryl will show you to your table. Champagne and some truly decadent desserts are on us, of course."

Ethan, seeming to realize he was holding up the line at the doors, nodded, gave Layla another glance that lasted a moment longer than it should have, then let the brunette—who was suddenly looking a lot happier with her job—lead him away. Layla watched him go, her thoughts tumbling.

Her greetings to the others were somewhat distracted, and she looked forward to the moment when she had to retreat backstage in preparation for the beginning of the evening's festivities. Once everyone had arrived and she was certain the initial serving was going well, she headed to the back of the room.

She had a moment to recover her poise and make another check in the mirror. Nothing had changed, except that she was oddly flushed. She knew she would be that way within minutes of being under the stage lights anyway, so she didn't worry. Nor did she allow herself to think of the cause.

She made her way out to the podium that sat off to one side, and right on cue the stage lights came on, drawing the crowd's attention. She swallowed, wishing she could leave this part of it to someone else. It wasn't that she was shy, but she wasn't comfortable being the center of attention for a group of hundreds.

She got through her introduction and the thank-yous on behalf of the Marina del Mar Alzheimer's Center well enough, she thought, and turned to introducing the emcee for the evening. It was someone new, a comedian from Laughlin, Nevada, whom Harry had found. She'd thought his credits a bit padded, but Harry had chosen him, so she hadn't questioned his decision.

Now she was simply glad when he came out and she could again retreat backstage. She had a few things to do: check with the kitchen to be sure things were running smoothly; make sure they'd stocked enough champagne and wine; check on the tracker's table, where they kept tabs on who bid what for whom; and touch base with the hotel staff, to head off any potential problems. Then she could once more retreat backstage, where everyone knew to find her if there was a problem.

Everything seemed to be going well, and after a brief chat with the maître d' they'd been assigned for the evening, she started walking along the side of the ballroom, heading toward the backstage door. She was passing the front tables when she felt an odd tickle at the back of her neck. She paused and looked, but there was no one close by. Then she noticed a turned head at one of the front tables and realized someone was watching her.

The stage light widened as the first of the auctionees came onto the stage. In the spillover light, she could now see the man whose gaze seemed fastened on her.

Ethan Winslow.

Instinctively she pulled back slightly. She couldn't be sure he could see that she'd noticed, but he must have seen that she'd stopped. She turned quickly and continued on her way, wondering. By the time she was backstage, she'd convinced herself he was regretting that he'd ever agreed to this and wanted to be sure he knew where she was so that he could take it out on her later.

She didn't relax until she was behind the curtain and sitting quietly in the chair she'd placed there earlier, in the perfect spot both to monitor the activity on stage and get a feel for what was happening out in the crowd.

She didn't, she realized after a few minutes, much care for Harry's choice of emcee. More than once, there was something in Marty Ruttles's jokes that bordered on cruel. Fortunately, it wasn't constant and probably wouldn't leave the audience with a sour taste.

She was delighted when Gloria's evening at a premiere musical, complete with celebrity party afterward, went quickly and for a very respectable amount. But then, she'd expected it; Charles Emerson, the bidder, had told her he'd had his sights set on Gloria for months now.

And she wasn't in the least surprised at the buzz that went around the room—among the females, at least—when Ethan took the stage, before Ruttles even announced what his planned evening was.

Ethan didn't look happy, but it didn't matter; nothing could detract from the impact of this man in a tuxedo. He could have proposed an evening of laying brick and Layla bet it would go in a rush. As it was, his offering of an evening at the upcoming grand opening of the new county museum of natural history—to be attended by a rather select group— only added to the anticipation.

The emcee urged the crowd to spend freely, to make the newcomer welcome, and opened the bidding. It went as quickly as she expected. Usually a newcomer to the process began to relax when he realized there were at least going to be bids, but Ethan didn't look any happier now than he had before. And when the bidding finally ended—with, Layla noted without surprise, the highest total so far—he seemed nothing more than grateful to escape.

She leaned back in her chair. If Ethan Winslow couldn't

relax, she certainly could. She was always relieved when a first timer's auction went well, and she told herself she was no more relieved than usual that his had.

Odd, she thought, she hadn't even noticed who had made the final bid. The amount limited who it could be, she supposed; there were only a few people in that bracket. She would have to ask. It was part of her job, after all, to be aware of such things, she told herself. She would have to do a press release on the results of the auction, and of course the highest bid would be included, and who made it. So she would have to know who had paid such a high price for an evening with Ethan Winslow.

It had nothing to do with her beyond that, she assured herself.

And realized she was doing a lot of that, telling herself things meant nothing, really.

She was so deep in her thoughts that she almost missed her cue to come back out to wrap things up. She always reserved the last minutes of the evening to personally thank everyone; she owed them that, even if she would rather walk on hot coals than go out there again. But there was nothing more important to her than this cause, so go she would, and do the best she could.

"—the reason this evening is what it is, the power behind the scenes, the dynamo who organized it all, got you all here and kept things running tonight..."

She was starting to get embarrassed; Ruttles apparently did everything to excess, including introductions. At last he said her name. She steeled herself, then stepped out onto the stage. The applause was gratifying, she supposed, but she still wanted this over with.

She headed for the emcee, her hand already rising to take the portable microphone, but she paused in puzzlement a foot away when Ruttles didn't move—in fact, held the microphone away from her.

The man looked at her with that too wide smile that had

so irritated her when she'd first met him. He lifted the microphone. Began to speak.

And stunned Layla breathless.

Shock filled her as his words penetrated. She stood motionless, as if rooted to the stage she'd never wanted to take. She stared at him, sure her face was registering her horror, but unable to help it.

Every old, self-conscious feeling she'd ever had about herself came roaring back, magnified into dread. This couldn't be happening, it couldn't....

But it was.

Ruttles was trying to auction *her* off.

Three

Ethan had never been so glad an evening was nearly over. Even the date that had been sold along with him couldn't be as awkward and uncomfortable as this had been.

He'd been engrossed in reading the program, which described the accomplishments of the sponsoring Alzheimer's center, when he heard Layla introduced. He had looked up as she crossed the stage. She walked like a queen, he thought rather inanely, head up, shoulders back. She didn't slump, didn't mince, didn't try to hide her size. And it wasn't that she was obese by any standard, she was just…big. A big, solid woman. With a definitely female shape. Her curves were generous but well-proportioned, her waist, well-defined, and what he could see of her legs, nicely shaped.

Layla Laraway was simply a lot of woman, and he had a feeling that was true in more ways than one.

He was honest enough to admit he'd been surprised at his first sight of her. And had immediately felt guilty for it; it wasn't her fault he'd pictured a petite, sultry brunette on the other end of the line. But what had disturbed him most was what he'd seen in her eyes, in her face.

She *knew*.

He'd thought about it as he let Cheryl, a woman who was almost exactly what he'd imagined the sexy-voiced Ms. Laraway would be, lead him to his seat. He hadn't paid the woman much attention, he feared, despite her stream of friendly chatter.

Of course she knew, he realized as he'd taken his seat. How could she not? She must have been faced with this before, the reaction from someone who'd only heard her and had done as he had, built some sort of image in his mind. It had shown in her face, in the sudden tension in her stance, and he didn't like thinking about what it must be like for her to go through that time and again.

She didn't move the way some of the larger women he'd known did. In fact, she moved like an athlete, in balance and graceful. And when she stopped, she simply stopped. She didn't strike a pose as many of the women this evening did. She simply stood, again in balance.

His gaze went back to her face.

He saw nothing short of mortification there.

Ethan abruptly tuned back in to what was happening. And once he realized that the long, painful silence he'd just tuned into was the result of the idiot emcee trying to auction off their hostess, he understood her look perfectly.

"She may be a great organizer, but I couldn't afford to feed her."

Ethan's head snapped around, and he stared at the man at the table behind him who had made the comment. The man had the grace to look abashed, then lowered his head and stared at his plate. A bid that was quite obviously a token, far below most of the rest of the evening, was called out.

Ethan's gaze shot back to Layla. She was still staring at the emcee in shock. But then she seemed to pull herself up and regain some of her poise. She reached for the microphone, and he could sense she was going to try to pass it off as a joke.

The emcee, apparently oblivious, laughingly held the microphone out of her reach.

Anger shot through Ethan. She'd put this whole thing together, she'd worked long and hard, she was utterly dedicated to this cause, and she deserved a hell of a lot better than to be treated this way.

And the next thing he knew, he was on his feet.

"I know it's too low for the woman who brought us all here tonight with her tireless efforts," he said, loudly enough to be heard across the room, "but I'll match the highest bid of the night."

Layla's head came around sharply. She stared at him, and he had the oddest feeling she wasn't particularly grateful for what he'd done.

"Well, well," said Ruttles. "A man who doesn't even care that she doesn't have a date prepared!"

"She organized this, didn't she?" Ethan said with a wide gesture toward the room. "I'm not worried." *You jerk,* he added silently.

A round of applause that seemed as much relieved as anything met his words, and he sat down.

Layla, brooking no further denial, finally wrested the microphone away from the suddenly wary emcee. But if she was angry, it didn't show in her voice as she thanked everyone for coming and promised that their contributions would be put to good use in the fight.

The lights went out. In the shadows, Ethan saw her set the microphone down on the podium and walk away. He stood, but waited until most of the crowd had filtered out, watching the stage door.

"Thank you, Mr. Winslow." Ethan turned to see the man who had greeted him at the door. Harry, he thought. "That could have been an awkward moment."

Ethan shrugged, not knowing what to say.

"I should have listened to Layla. She said she didn't like the guy."

Good judgment, Ethan thought.

Harry thanked him again, then bustled away. Ethan waited. And waited. The lights went down in the room, and the hotel staff, who were already cleaning up, cast glances at him.

He finally left without ever seeing Layla again.

"I've been more humiliated in my life, but not in the last ten years." Layla stabbed at her salad rather viciously.

"Sounds to me like the proverbial prince on a white horse rode in and rescued you."

Layla slanted a look across the table at Stephanie Parker.

"Hey," her best friend said, "who cares how it happened. Just enjoy."

Layla grimaced. "You only say that because you haven't seen him."

Stephanie set down her own fork, then looked at Layla intently. Her friend, Layla thought, was exactly the kind of woman you would expect to see Ethan Winslow with. Normal height, with thick, glossy dark hair cut in a short, chic bob, a slim, shapely figure and a glamorous look that could have graced any magazine cover. And on top of that, she had brains; she was a vice president at one of the biggest ad agencies in the county.

But beneath all the glamour was the most steadfast, loyal friend Layla had ever had. They had connected in the third grade—before Layla had begun the spurt of growth that had left Stephanie far behind—and been the closest of friends ever since.

"So," Stephanie said now, "how gorgeous is he?"

"The kind that's usually spoken in conjunction with the words 'drop dead,'" she said wryly.

Stephanie grinned. "Good girl!"

Of course, Stephanie didn't understand. How could she?

She'd never in her life been anything less than beautiful. She doubted if Ethan Winslow had ever been, either.

"I'll have to look up his name," Stephanie said.

It was a hobby of Stephanie's; she loved to analyze how people matched or contradicted the meaning of their name. Layla, Stephanie had told her years ago, was a variation on the Middle English Leala, which meant loyal.

"So where are you going to take him?"

Layla sighed. "I'm not."

"But he bid—"

"It was charity, Steph."

"Well, of course. The whole thing was for charity."

"I mean what he did was charity. Out of pity."

"He told you that?"

"Well, no."

"What did he tell you?"

Layla shifted in her seat. "Nothing. I…haven't talked to him."

Stephanie's dark, perfectly arched brows rose. "You haven't talked to him since Saturday night?"

"I took yesterday off. I always take the Monday after the auction off, you know that. And I haven't been into the office yet today."

"And you…what, forgot his phone number?"

"It's on my desk. At work," Layla clarified. Sometimes Stephanie was like a bulldog, never letting go. And now she was studying Layla as if she were one of her proposed ad layouts.

"So tell me, girlfriend," Stephanie drawled, "who are you hiding from? Him, or yourself?"

"Both," Layla admitted. "But with reason. It would be…silly to expect him to keep that promise, when it was made essentially under duress."

Stephanie sighed aloud. "So, you think he's one of those? Like Wayne?"

Layla grimaced. This was the problem with friends who

had known you forever, they knew too much. She'd tried her best to forget Wayne Doucet, who had been the architect of both the highest and lowest days of her life. The highest had been when, at her thinnest, he'd proposed to her. The lowest had come after her hospital stay, when she had regained some of the weight she'd forced herself to lose, and gotten back to what her doctor had told her was a healthy weight for her. Wayne had dropped hints about her "porking up," as he'd called it, and when she finally told him that this was her natural weight and she couldn't fight it anymore, he had walked out. But not before saying he thought she'd better give him back the ring he'd bought her—if she could get it off.

"I don't think there's *anybody* like Wayne," she muttered.

"Oh, I'm sure they're out there," Stephanie said. "But it usually takes longer than two minutes face-to-face to ferret them out."

Layla flushed. "I don't really think he's…like that."

"Then why are you running?"

"I'm not," she said. "I'm just…giving him time, so he knows it's not important, that I don't really expect him to do it."

"So you do think he'd hold your size against you?"

Layla sighed; Stephanie was clearly in full bulldog mode. "I was watching his face when he first saw me. He was better and quicker at hiding it than most, but it was there."

She knew she didn't have to explain. Stephanie had been through enough with her over the years. And one of the things Layla loved most about her was her honest outrage at the way Layla was sometimes treated. She could almost feel it bubbling up in her old friend right now.

On the thought, Stephanie spoke and proved her right. "You're a smart, dynamic, intelligent woman! And whether you believe it or not, you're beautiful. It's the men who can't see that who have the problem."

Impulsively, Layla reached across the table and clasped

her friend's hand. "And you're the best friend anybody could ever have."

"Humph. You didn't say that when I broke your bike," Stephanie said.

Layla grinned, glad Stephanie was at least smiling. "Nor you when I broke your brand-new Walkman before you'd even had a chance to listen to it."

They both laughed then. It was an old joke with them, had been for a long time, so long that it had become a signal of sorts. On the rare occasions when they did argue, if either of them felt things were getting out of hand, too close to permanent damage being done, those were the code words. Layla had only to say "Bike breaker," or Stephanie to say "Walkman wrecker," and the fight was over.

Stephanie had always told her that someday she would meet the man who would love her for herself. Layla had always laughed it off, but somewhere deep inside she had hoped her friend was right. That someday that man might happen along. But there was no doubt in her mind that, no matter how appealing the thought might be, a man like Ethan Winslow wasn't him.

"You're a hard woman to track down."

Layla whirled, almost knocking over her desk chair. Ethan Winslow was standing in her office doorway, lounging against the doorjamb rather nonchalantly.

"I...hello. I just got here."

He nodded toward her desk. "A couple of those messages are from me."

"Sorry," she said. "I usually take some time off after...the auction."

"I can understand that. It's...quite a production. And things like that don't go as smoothly as that one did without a heck of a lot of work."

"Thank you," she said; most people didn't think that much about what went on behind the scenes. But she didn't think he'd come here just to acknowledge that; no doubt he was here to make sure there was no misunderstanding, that she didn't expect him to really follow through on that bid.

"Come in," she said, belatedly remembering her manners.

He did, grabbed the single chair opposite her desk and sat. He waited until she also took her seat before speaking.

"So," he said with a crooked grin that made her pulse speed up a bit, "where are you taking me?"

So many answers to that raced through her mind that she clamped her jaw to be sure her mouth stayed shut. She had a moment to be grateful she was already seated. After a moment's desperate thinking, she came up with the perfect diversion.

"I forgot to check and see...who was your winning bidder?"

She realized, as he lifted a brow, that she'd betrayed her interest by her words, but he answered easily enough. "Gloria Van Alden. I gather she's quite the mover and shaker in town."

Layla's nervousness vanished. "Gloria? Lucky you! She's been everywhere, has the most marvelous stories, and she's a delightful person, to boot. You'll have a wonderful time."

He smiled at her, so warmly it almost made her blush. "That's the impression I got when I spoke to her."

"You don't mind that she's...a mature woman?"

His smile faded. "Why would I? I'm not looking to marry her, not that it would matter if I was. Besides, she's younger in the ways that count than a lot of women my age."

He sounded insulted, Layla thought. She liked the fact that that was his first reaction. She wasn't quite sure why, but assumed it was for Gloria's sake.

"So, where are you taking me? And when?"

Layla sighed. "Look, Mr. Winslow—"

"Ethan, please. If we're going out on a date, we should at least be on a first-name basis, don't you think, *Ms. Laraway?*"

No, Layla thought, *sometimes I don't think at all....*

"Ethan, then. And Layla, please. I want you to know how much I...appreciate what you did."

"Do you?" He leaned back in the chair and steepled his hands in front of him. "I got the impression that night that you wished I'd kept my mouth shut."

Startled by his perception, Layla admitted, "I was hoping to just make it go away, treat it like the joke it should have been."

"I don't think he would have let you."

Something in the way he said the "he" made her feel absurdly warmed. And gave her the nerve to go on. "That aside, I do appreciate it. But please understand, I never expected you to actually go through with it."

And she didn't. She knew perfectly well that he'd done it out of pity, or sympathy, or some equally repellent emotion. But he seemed a kind enough man, and she truly appreciated that he could be moved to act in such a situation.

"I never lie, and I always keep my word, Ms. Laraway."

"I'm sure you do, but this is...different."

"Why?"

"Because it never should have happened in the first place."

"Granted." He looked at her steadily. "If you can't stand even a single evening with me, just say so."

Layla gaped at him. How could he imagine any woman would think such a thing? "I...of course not."

"Okay. Then where are we going?"

She looked at him this time with genuine curiosity. "Why? You didn't even want to do the auction in the first place."

"That was different, and it doesn't mean I don't support the cause. It's important to me. Very important. And I made a bid in good faith."

He seemed determined. To finish his good deed, she supposed. Perhaps she should just let him. She became aware she was tapping a pen she didn't even remember picking up from her desk calendar. She set the pen down.

"I...don't have a plan. I never thought you were serious."

He didn't argue with her again. "You've been doing this for years, right? You must have thought about what your idea of the ideal auction package would be."

"What appeals to me wouldn't necessarily appeal to some of the high rollers we pull in."

"That's their problem," he said, obviously not including himself in the high-roller class, although Layla knew he qualified financially. "What would you choose?"

"Oh, something silly." Her own words about high rollers triggered the only thing she could think of at the moment. "Like a trip to the highest, fastest roller coaster in the state."

He grinned suddenly. "I love roller coasters."

That grin should be registered as a weapon, Layla thought ruefully. With a conscious effort, she pulled herself together. It wasn't like her to be this flustered by anyone, let alone a man, and she wasn't going to start now. She looked at him thoughtfully.

"Or," she said, "a sailboat trip to Catalina Island for lunch."

"Great, let's do it." The grin widened. "I learned to sail in the Boy Scouts."

Layla rolled her eyes and groaned theatrically. "A Boy Scout? You were a Boy Scout?"

"Guilty, I'm afraid."

"Merit badges?"

"Several."

"Camp-outs?"

"Those, too."

Layla shook her head in feigned shock. "Oh, dear. I just don't know, that sounds far too...normal."

"Would you feel better if I said I quit when I was sixteen?"

"Maybe. Being kicked out would be better."

Ethan laughed, a deep, hearty laugh that made Layla laugh, too. And suddenly she realized that she would enjoy spending time with him, even knowing it would be merely a one-time obligation on his part.

I'm not looking to marry her....

He knew it was only an auction date. How often had she reassured participants it was nothing more than a few hours spent on an enjoyable activity with someone who cared about a cause just as you did? Maybe she should take her own advice.

Who cares how it happens? Just enjoy.

Stephanie's words echoed in her mind. True, Stephanie didn't truly understand the problem, but that didn't mean it wasn't good advice, too.

And for once, she was going to take it.

"I have a friend whose family has a sailboat," she said. "I've sailed with them enough times that I think they'd trust me with it."

"It's a date," Ethan said, still grinning. "When?"

"Your choice. A weekend day would be best, I presume?"

She couldn't believe she was going ahead with it. But now that she'd said it, now that she'd committed to it out loud, she felt an odd, unfamiliar sense of excitement and anticipation.

They agreed on next Sunday, and once it was done, Layla found herself mentally calculating how much time she had to drive herself crazy over the idea. She wouldn't back out, not now that she'd agreed to it, but she knew there would be times over the next few days when she would wish she could.

"Layla?"

She looked up toward her doorway, where the young college student who helped around the office stood, clutching a manila envelope to her chest. Ethan stood, so smoothly and naturally that Layla knew it was automatic, and the girl's eyes widened. Her gaze flicked from him to Layla.

"Yes, Missy?" Layla asked, smiling; the girl was very

shy, so she was always careful to be welcoming and encouraging. The girl smiled back, taking the encouragement and stepping into the office.

"I—I'm glad I caught you before you left. Mr. Chandler wanted to know if you could take this with you. It's the memo on the funding for adult day-care at The Oaks."

"Of course." She took the envelope the girl held out. "Thank you."

The girl nodded and scuttled out of the room. Ethan watched her go curiously. "Is she always that nervous, or was it me?"

Layla gave him points for noticing—and for good manners—even as she warned herself to remember this man's perceptiveness. "She's just very shy. Especially around men."

"Oh." He turned back to her. "You have an appointment?"

"Of sorts. At The Oaks, the Alzheimer's board-and-care home. I go a couple of times a week." She added the folder to the small stack of papers she had ready to go. And then, impulsively, she asked, "Would you like to go? See where a lot of the money you earned for us goes?"

"No."

It was short, almost rudely sharp, and she looked up at him in surprise. He seemed to realize what he'd sounded like, because when he spoke again, his voice was more normal.

"Sorry."

But his jaw was still clenched, his lips tight. There had been a time when she would have assumed his reaction was to her temerity in even asking him, but she'd grown up since then. Besides, he didn't seem to be the type; he would hardly have forced the issue of their auction date and then take offense at this.

"What's wrong?" she asked.

"Nothing." It was sharp again, and she heard him take a

deep breath before he went on. "I just don't go to that place."

His vehemence startled her. She'd run into it before, she even understood it, but she hadn't expected it here. In most cases, she knew it was a natural dislike of facing the reality of Alzheimer's. But she had been at this long enough to sense that this was different. She recognized the feeling, the attitude, the anger, the guilt.

This was personal.

She wondered who was at The Oaks that Ethan Winslow didn't want to see.

Four

————

Ethan had given up trying to figure out all the reasons why he had made that bid. He supposed it was all tangled up with his feelings about being up on that stage himself, and how alone it had felt, an empathy drilled into him by his two sisters—both of whom had fought their own battles with weight over the years—and the vision of the lively, amusing woman he'd come to know over the phone placed in a humiliating position.

There were probably more reasons, gut-level things he didn't even realize, but he wasn't going to worry about them. It didn't matter now, anyway; it was done, and he didn't waste time dwelling on done deals. And now that the day was here—the early morning, he amended to himself—he planned on enjoying something he hadn't taken time for in years.

He had once loved sailing, had loved the feeling of freedom, being moved across the water by nothing more than the power of the wind in the sails. He'd been young then, and carefree. Oh, he hadn't thought so then—he'd been subject to the same intense angst as any other teenager, convinced his troubles were worse than anyone else's, and that no one could possibly understand them. But on the water he'd felt not just happy, but joyous.

And then he'd lost that joy and been shown brutally just what real trouble was.

He shook his head at his unaccustomed lingering on the past, yanked on his athletic shoes—his old boat shoes had long since gone—grabbed a baseball cap from a doorknob, a light jacket from the hall tree, and was out the door.

An hour later they were casting off in the neat twenty-seven-foot sloop, heading for the Marina del Mar channel that would take them to the open sea. He was a little rusty, but it was coming back quickly. And Layla clearly had as much experience as she'd said; she moved quickly, efficiently and with easy familiarity, pulling canvas covers off the cockpit and sails, opening the hatch into the cabin and starting the marine diesel.

"I don't think I'm quite up to sailing out or back into the channel yet," she'd said with a laugh. "We'll leave that to experts like Stephanie's father and motor out."

"Fine with me," Ethan agreed. Once he might have tried it. But once he'd been young and cocky and sure he could do anything.

He brushed aside old memories and focused on today. He'd met her at the marina. She'd given him the slip number, and she'd been easy enough to spot; she was, after all, a tall woman. She'd been wearing a long, soft green lightweight sweater—she burned easily, she'd said, so long sleeves and sunblock were a requisite on a summer day on the water—dark pants and deck shoes. Her hair was tucked neatly up under a matching green sun hat, her eyes shaded by wraparound sunglasses. She'd hardly dressed up for the day, but she looked neat, practical and comfortable. He liked that;

he'd seen too many women who were more concerned about appearance than practicality, and ended up suffering for it.

He'd cast off the lines and jumped back aboard, then pulled up the rubber fenders that kept the boat from rubbing against the sides of the slip. It felt good, having a deck beneath him again, and he wondered why he'd let this thing he'd once loved so much slip out of his life.

He checked out the boat, learning where everything was, while Layla motored them slowly down the channel. The *Willow* was a fixed-keel sloop, she'd told him, named after Stephanie and her brother's favorite childhood tale, *The Wind in the Willows*. It was an older boat, but exquisitely kept, and Ethan guessed the family had logged many a nautical mile in the vessel.

Once they cleared the breakwater, Ethan felt the surge as the first swell lifted them. He couldn't help smiling, and in that moment Layla looked over at him, and he saw she, too, was smiling, with eagerness, with the same joy he'd once felt to be free. An odd sense of excitement shot through him; he had, it seemed, missed this more than he'd realized.

When they were far enough out from the breakwater and away from the other boats taking advantage of this sunny Sunday, Layla turned them head-on into the wind and throttled back, leaving them just enough power to hold position.

"You want to hold us here or raise sail?" she asked.

"I'll do the sails," he said, adding with a grin, "If I remember how."

"Hasn't changed much," she said.

He gestured toward the bow. "I don't know. That's new to me."

"Roller furling?" she asked, referring to the roller system that allowed for neatly rolling the jib around its stay. "It sure beats having to drag the thing out of a sail bag and hook it up every time."

"I can see that," he said with a grin as he stepped up on the roof of the cabin and began to hoist the mainsail. It went up smoothly, and the sound of the flapping canvas—or whatever they were making them of these days—was like an old favorite tune, forgotten until you heard it again, but then welcomed eagerly.

When both sails were set, he rejoined her in the cockpit. She turned the big silver wheel slightly, edging the boat around. The sails flapped more loudly as they went, the trailing edge of the mainsail rippling wildly.

And then the wind bellied out the sails, and the boat rose to the wind like a bird, heeling over slightly in the medium breeze. When the sails were full, without a trace of flutter, Layla straightened the wheel.

"Atta girl," she murmured to the boat.

"Girl?" he asked teasingly.

"That's a centuries-old tradition I'm not about to fight," she said with a sideways grin. "I prefer to pick battles I can win. Besides, it's rather flattering, in a way."

"I'm sure it was meant to be," he said, looking out over the bow.

"Ready to cut the motor?"

Something in her voice as she asked made him look at her again, and he knew the moment he saw her face that she was as eager as he was to cut off the steady thrum of the diesel and let the wind take over completely.

In answer, he reached over and turned the key to Off. The motor died away obediently. And there it was, what Ethan had always loved best about sailing, the exhilarating silence, the sound of wind power only. There were other boats around, powerboats with their noisy motors, but out here they seemed far away, leaving them and the *Willow* to the joy of the wind.

"Want to take over?" Layla asked.

"You trust me?"

"You seem to be remembering pretty well."

"Some things you don't forget," he said.

She released the wheel to him. He gripped the stainless

steel, felt the leaping power of the wind translated into motion shivering through the metal. He found himself grinning
widely. He looked at Layla, who was smiling at him. And
suddenly everything he'd left behind in his office, all the
problems, all the worry slipped away as cleanly as if a mooring line had been severed.

And the world seemed very, very right.

Layla was rather proud of herself. She'd made up her mind
to quash her nervousness and enjoy the day, and so far she'd
done just that. When she'd left the house this morning, she'd
been reluctant and oddly excited at the same time, but finally
her common sense, which told her repeatedly that he was
doing this out of duty, won out, and she relaxed.

Of course, Ethan had made it easy; he had obviously loved
the sail over to Catalina Island, and although he'd been a
little tentative at first, it soon became clear that he had sailed
before. More than once he had moved to make an adjustment
in course or sail that she'd been about to do herself, and soon
she was able to relax and not think anymore about the expensive toy Stephanie's family had entrusted her with, to relax and enjoy the surprisingly easy camaraderie they had
dropped into.

And more than once she'd caught herself watching him. It
had been too tempting to resist from safely behind her nicely
dark sunglasses. She'd watched him move with a centered
grace over the decks of the *Willow,* watched him grin along
with her as a pair of porpoises took a ride on their bow wave.
And there was a moment when he'd been standing near the
bow, when he'd pulled off his cap and let the wind whip his
hair, when he'd leaned back and turned his face to the sun,
when her breath had almost stopped.

God, he's beautiful, she'd thought.

And now, looking across the restaurant table at him, she
saw no reason to change that assessment. She couldn't quite
believe how easily she'd talked to him on the sail over, how

effortless it had been to carry on a lighthearted conversation; looking at him now, she was amazed she'd even been able to form a coherent sentence.

"—thank them for me. I'd forgotten how much I love sailing."

Layla jerked herself out of her reverie. "I'll tell them. But I think simply bringing the boat back in one piece will suffice."

"That's a lot of trust," he said.

Layla nodded, then smiled. "Mr. Parker taught me to sail himself, so that helps."

Ethan smiled back. "He must have been a good teacher."

"He was. And he's a great sailor. It's his passion."

"Everyone should have a passion," he said.

Layla was thankful he wasn't looking at her when he said that; she was certain the things that leaped into her mind at his words must show on her face. Quickly she scrambled for something else to say.

"He has a sailing saying for everything. And he's the only person I know who actually knows what 'three sheets to the wind' really means."

"I know a sheet isn't the sail but the rope attached to a sail," Ethan said with a laugh. "But dare I ask?"

"On the old sailing ships, there was a sheet at each corner of the sails. When one came loose, it caused an imbalance in the way the ship sailed," she recited dutifully. "If two came loose, the skipper started to lose control. If a third came loose, the ship went nuts, reeling and circling."

"Hence 'three sheets to the wind' meaning drunk," Ethan said, still laughing.

"Exactly." Layla felt relaxed again. "Even his philosophy of life was a sailing-ism. He always said, 'If you want to be happy, try to change the sail, not the wind.'"

"He sounds like a wise man."

"He is. He's why Stephanie is who she is, instead of who she could have become."

He lifted a brow at her. "Interesting way to put it."

"Stephanie's been my best friend since the third grade, and she's the most beautiful woman I know. She's also the most unspoiled beautiful woman I know."

He looked at her curiously. To her surprise, he didn't ask anything about Stephanie. He finished a bite of his fresh albacore salad sandwich before asking, "You've always lived here in Marina del Mar, then?"

"Pretty much. My dad went to work at the university in Irvine when I was four."

She didn't think her voice had changed, but his gaze seemed to sharpen. "He's a professor?"

"He was. He died five years ago."

She felt the same tug of sadness, of loss, that she always felt when speaking of her father. The raw, ripping grief had finally passed, although it had taken a very long time.

"I'm sorry," he said.

She braced herself for more, for the usual sympathy offering, but it didn't come. When she met his eyes, she saw it all there, sympathy, empathy and a knowledge that told her he knew how she felt.

"So am I," she answered quietly. "But he…left long before he died."

He didn't miss her phrasing, or the implication. "Alzheimer's?" he guessed.

She nodded. "He was brilliant. Some of his treatises are still in use as texts for college courses all over the country."

She saw something stir in his eyes, something deep and dark that flickered and was gone. "It must have been terrible for your family."

"There was only him and me by then. But it was…horrible. To see that mind, that genius, degenerate until he was almost helpless… He would get lost a block from home. Look at the photograph of my mother and ask who she was. The next day think I was her." She shook her head sharply as the memories threatened to overwhelm her poise.

"I was lucky, he never got violent, just...childlike. I was able to keep him at home."

Again something flickered in his eyes, and he spoke quickly, before she could go on. "So that's why you do what you do?"

She nodded. "The fewer people who have to go through what I did, the better. Dad left me well enough off that I can devote my time to it. It seems only right." She took a sip of her iced tea. It was time, she thought, to change the tide here; she'd talked enough about herself. She took another sip of her iced tea before changing the subject.

"So how long have you lived here?"

"All my life."

Surprised, she asked, "You went to Marina del Mar High? How'd I miss that?"

"I must have been a few years ahead of you."

She sat back slightly. "You couldn't have been that far ahead."

He smiled. "Thanks. But I'm thirty-five."

"Oh. Then you would have graduated the year I started."

His smile widened. "Not coy about your age, are you?"

She shrugged. "Hitting my thirties wasn't particularly traumatic for me. I make no promises about forty, though," she added with a laugh. They were back on her again, and she determinedly changed the tack. "Do you have family here?"

He nodded. "My two little sisters." With a grin he added, "I only call them that because it makes them crazy, since they're twenty-eight and thirty."

She smiled. "What are their names?"

"Margaret-don't-ever-call-me-Maggie, and Sarah."

She laughed then. "Why do I sense a teasing big brother in there somewhere?"

"Guilty," he admitted. "But she used to make me so crazy."

"It's in the younger sibling job description, I think."

He laughed. "After I hit about ten, I often wished to be an only child."

"It's overrated," she said frankly. "Wouldn't you have missed them, really?"

He suddenly went very still. "Yes," he said quietly. "I would."

Something low and dark had come into his voice, and his eyes had gone distant, unfocused, as if he were looking at some place—or some time—far away. Layla couldn't stop herself from asking, "Ethan? What is it?"

"They tried to take them away," he said in a voice that matched that distant look. "After our folks were killed in a car crash when I was seventeen. There weren't any relatives, so they were going to split us up."

"How awful!" She might not have had siblings of her own, but she could imagine how it must have felt. Losing her parents one at a time had been bad enough, but at least she'd had her father until adulthood. To have been orphaned so instantly...

He shook his head sharply, coming back from where he'd been with a snap that was almost audible. "Sorry," he muttered.

About what? she wondered. Remembering? Or telling her, an almost stranger? It seemed obvious he wasn't used to talking about it, so she had to assume he regretted telling her. But she couldn't help asking, "What happened?"

"It worked out. They stayed with me." He said it shortly, clearly unwilling to dwell on it.

My God, Layla thought to herself, he'd done that? He'd taken on two little girls by himself?

He was watching her as if wary about what she would say. She wondered why. What was there to say except that it was a wonderful, loving, incredible thing that he'd done?

It hit her then that that just might be what he was wary of. Perhaps he'd been told it so often he didn't want to hear it anymore. Maybe it was his "You'd be beautiful if..."

So she didn't say it. Instead she asked, "Where are your sisters now?"

"Margaret's up in Orange. She's a pediatrician, just starting her own practice, near Children's Hospital. She's married to a child psychologist."

"Handy," Layla said with a smile.

But she was also realizing what that casual statement meant: four years of college, four years of medical school. Had he paid for it all? And maybe helped support her through years of pediatric residency after that?

"And Sarah?" she asked instead, realizing it wasn't really her business.

"Sarah's still here in Marina del Mar," he said. "She's working for a local radio station as a newswriter."

Layla leaned back in her chair and looked across the table at him. "Well," she said with a quirk of her mouth, "I can see they suffered irreparable harm being raised by you."

He looked startled; then he smiled. A warm, gentle smile that transformed him from a strikingly handsome man to a very, very human one. "I'm proud of them both."

"And yourself, I hope."

He shrugged. "That's what Sarah keeps saying. But they did it themselves. And we all pitched in, after…the accident. I didn't do it alone."

"They sound like my kind of people," she said.

He seemed to consider that for a moment. "Yes, I think they would be."

Feeling complimented—oddly, since she'd said it first—Layla picked up her glass of iced tea and sipped again. Lunch had been delicious, and she hadn't once had the feeling Ethan was watching her eat. Some people did, as if they were policing her. She knew perfectly well that she ate no more than most people did, she was simply, as her doctor put it, the kind of person whose metabolism could efficiently survive a food shortage. But Ethan hadn't even blinked or commented beyond asking her how her food was when it had arrived.

They'd walked around the waterfront after they'd reached shore on the little water taxi that picked them up from the mooring. Before eating, they'd made the requisite visit to the casino, the big, white, round landmark that made Avalon harbor so recognizable. And now they had a couple of hours left before they needed to start back, so she asked him what he wanted to do.

"It's been so long since I've been here, I don't know. Any ideas?"

She thought for a moment. "We could try and find the buffalo, I suppose." The small buffalo herd was famous for its unexpected presence here on the island. "Or go up to the cemetery, if you like that kind of thing."

"That I remember, as a kid," he said. "I could never figure out what people found so fascinating about a place full of dead people."

Layla laughed. "Remember the turnstiles that counted visitors? I always wondered what they did if one more went out than came in."

Ethan laughed loudly, drawing looks from around the small restaurant, curious from the men and—she couldn't deny it—appreciative from the women. And she also couldn't deny that the looks usually went from him to her and quickly changed to anything from questioning to disbelieving.

Suddenly her patience with that kind of thing ran out; she didn't want anything intruding on the perfection of this day. "Have you ever been to the Zane Grey house?"

"No," he answered, looking interested. "But I remember reading my dad's copies of his books when I was a kid. I liked them."

"So do I. It's not too far away," she said. "We should have just enough time."

"Let's go, then," he said, and stood.

Since it was her date, and he was paying far too much for it anyway, she paid the bill and was grateful when he didn't quibble.

But the feeling faded when she noticed the look of sudden understanding from one of the men who had been glancing at them earlier; clearly he thought this was the only way she could get a man like Ethan to spend time with her.

She tried to quash her reaction. It didn't matter what this stranger thought, she told herself. It only mattered what Ethan thought, and he certainly didn't seem to be bothered to be seen with her.

Of course, he also knew it was only for today.

It took all of her determination to regain her earlier happy mood.

Five

Ethan lolled on the cushioned cockpit bench in the sun, watching Layla competently handle the sloop. He couldn't remember the last time he'd felt so relaxed. In fact, he couldn't remember the last time he'd spent most of a day, even a weekend day, without a thought of work.

It wasn't because of the beer she'd pulled out of the small galley fridge for him; he hadn't even finished it yet, although they'd set sail well over an hour ago. Nor was it because of the gorgeous weather; he was used to this, the endless string of sun-drenched southern California days.

It was because it wasn't really a date, of course. He'd never realized how much pressure being in a dating situation put on you, especially a first date. Which this wasn't, thankfully. If it was, he might be sitting here wondering how he was coming across, instead of simply admiring the way she was handling the boat.

If it was a date, he thought ruefully, he wouldn't have blurted out his pitiful life story.

He couldn't believe he'd done that. He never talked about that time, or what had happened, at least not voluntarily. He supposed he should have been more on guard; she'd already talked him into doing something he would have sworn he would never do in his life. Anybody who could manage that could coax out deeper secrets than his family history, if there were any.

Not that she'd had to coax much, he admitted. And not that it was a secret; he simply didn't talk about it. He'd long ago grown uncomfortable with the usual reaction, the need most people had to confer on him some kind of nobility for simply doing what had to be done.

But Layla hadn't done that. That familiar expression had come over her face, as if she'd been thinking what everybody seemed to think, and he'd been braced to deflect the praise he didn't want, to try to explain that there had been no other option; to tear his family apart when it had already been devastated by the death of both parents had not been an acceptable choice.

But instead she had asked about his sisters and, in a subtle, teasing way he could accept, complimented him on how they had turned out.

The *Willow* cut through a larger swell, leaping forward a little as she came down the other side. Layla never faltered, barely swayed on her feet. She'd offered him the wheel again, but he'd grinned and declined, saying he was feeling lazy. Which was true, but he also enjoyed watching her; he appreciated competence, in whatever form he found it.

He glanced back over his shoulder at the sun as Layla guided them home. She'd timed it almost perfectly; they should be back at the slip before it was too dark to see to break down the boat. He straightened and went back to watching her.

She had, he decided after a while, about the cutest nose he'd seen in a while. Narrow and turned up just slightly at the tip. Sort of like Sarah's. Of course, growing up, Sarah had always bemoaned it, saying her nose was disgustingly perky, when she wanted sexy. At the time Ethan had told her soberly—with an effort—that he wasn't sure noses were way up there on the sexiness list, anyway.

But this one could be, he thought rather dreamily as he downed the last swallow of beer, by now a little too warm for his taste. But if you really wanted sexy, try that mouth. It definitely qualified. Full and perfectly shaped, it begged to be kissed, and often. It—

He jerked upright, startled at the unexpected, inexplicable and unwanted direction his thoughts had taken. Drawn by his sudden movement, Layla looked back at him.

"Almost dropped the bottle," he muttered, got up and quickly headed for the hatchway. He went down the steep stairs and deposited the empty in the sink they'd cleaned out when they docked.

And for a moment he stayed there, wondering what the hell had brought on that bit of idiocy. Hadn't he just been enjoying the fact that this wasn't a date?

Besides, she was hardly his type. He went for brunettes, mostly. Exotic, sultry types. The kind of woman he'd pictured Layla to be, from her voice on the phone.

He knew he was dodging the real issue. He felt uncomfortable even thinking about it, acknowledging it, because she was smart, witty, charming, dedicated....

Sounds like somebody trying to sell you on a blind date who's a dog.

Bill Stanley's words came back to him, and they seemed even colder and crueler now than they had then. Layla was hardly a dog. She was just...bigger than he'd imagined. Not that it seemed to hinder her much. She moved easily and swiftly, and she was obviously fit, strong and healthy; it showed in everything she did.

And she *was* smart, witty, charming, dedicated and all the rest of those things. Besides, he liked her. She was fun to be with, and he enjoyed the way her quick, intelligent mind worked. And since this wasn't a romantic date, that was all that mattered, he told himself firmly, and turned and headed back up on deck.

"You should have your own boat," he said to her as he went to stand beside her at the wheel.

"I'd love to, but I just don't have enough time for the upkeep."

He nodded in understanding. "I remember my sailing instructor saying it was two hours of work for every hour spent sailing."

"Unless it's a wooden boat, in which case the labor increases exponentially."

He chuckled. "Yeah. You pay for all that character."

"Life in a nutshell. Character can cost." She gave him a sideways look and a quirky smile that made him smile back.

"I hadn't thought about it like that." She did that a lot, turned a simple thing sideways into a philosophical observation that made him think. "So you think you pay a price for character? For integrity?"

She thought for a moment. "Being a person of integrity costs you sometimes, yes. Of course, nothing's always black and white, but unless you had no choice, I think the price you'd pay for going the other way, even though it's easier, would be higher in the end."

"Because you'd destroy that character and integrity."

She nodded. He didn't say anything more. There didn't seem to be anything more to say. There was, it seemed, a lot to admire about Layla Laraway.

He tried to recall the last time he'd carried on such a varied conversation with a woman—with anyone, for that matter—outside of his work. Occasionally serious, frequently amusing and always interesting. And laugh-inducing. He'd laughed more today than he had in a long time. And it felt good. Maybe his sisters *were* right: his life had become too narrow, too lonely, too single track.

He remembered the day Sarah had moved out. He hadn't

quite understood her need to have a place of her own, when their house wasn't all that far from her work and they had plenty of room for the two of them, since Margaret had left after her marriage. But she had an independent streak that had made him crazy, sometimes with irritation, sometimes with worry, from the time she'd become his responsibility, and he knew better than to try to change her mind once it was made up.

But he'd felt so lost that day, standing there in the empty house he'd fought so hard to keep. Although their parents' insurance had paid off the mortgage, he'd had to work steadily to pay the taxes and keep the girls in decent clothes and provide a luxury or two. Not that they hadn't pitched in to help, Margaret with a part-time job at a department store, and even young Sarah with a seemingly never-ending series of enterprises, from a paper route to baby-sitting to dog-walking.

But the main responsibility had been his, and when it was suddenly over, he hadn't quite known what to do with himself. So he'd poured all that energy and attention into his work. It had worked insofar as to bring him success, even a measure of wealth, but it had also become his life, as his friends—and both his sisters—were wont to tell him at every opportunity. Laughter was something he didn't seem to have time for anymore.

Until today.

No, he amended silently, that wasn't quite right. Layla had had him laughing the very first time she'd called him on the phone. And that hadn't changed, even though she hadn't turned out to be exactly the woman he had pictured.

She could still make him laugh. And that, he thought, feeling a little silly, made him smile.

It had been, Layla thought, a lovely day. Darn near perfect, in fact.

She lounged back in the overstuffed chair that was her

favorite spot in her bright, cheerful living room, sipping occasionally at the last of the glass of wine she'd had with dinner. She was pleasantly tired after a day in the sun and fresh air. She'd managed not to get sunburned, the sail over to the island had presented no real problems, the tour of Zane Grey's home had been fascinating, the sail back had been smooth and even quicker thanks to the increased afternoon breeze, and they had left the *Willow* spotless and tightly buttoned up.

They.

It had definitely been they. Ethan had worked as hard as she had to tidy the boat and leave everything exactly as they'd found it. He'd had the fun, he said, so he would clean up. And it did seem that he'd had fun, she thought. She didn't think he was pretending. He didn't seem the type to do that, especially for an entire day.

The ringing of her phone interrupted her musings. Stephanie, she thought, no doubt checking to see how it had gone. She'd been more excited than Layla herself, it had seemed.

When she picked up the receiver, before she could even say hello, she was proved right.

"How did it go?"

"The boat's fine, no dings, nice and clean and tidy, and back in her cozy little slip," Layla said, knowing perfectly well that that wasn't what Stephanie wanted to know.

"Brat," her friend said briefly. "You know what I mean."

"Fine," Layla said, relenting. "It was a beautiful day."

"I wasn't asking about the weather, either."

"I know."

Stephanie's voice brightened. "That good?"

"I had a wonderful time. And he didn't hate it."

"Of course he didn't. What's to hate?"

"Well, it was hardly the kind of day worth his ridiculous bid."

"Did he say that?"

Stephanie sounded suddenly tense, as if she were going on

the offensive, and Layla hastened to defend Ethan from her loyal friend.

"No, he didn't. He said it was...perfect. Just the kind of day he'd pick himself."

"You sound surprised."

"I suppose I am. Everyone says what a mover and shaker he is, on his way up even further, and it seems like too simple a day for someone like him."

"And who says you're not a mover and shaker?" Stephanie asked, instantly jumping to her defense, as usual. "You accomplish more in this town than some so-called high-powered execs."

Layla knew it was useless arguing that point with her friend, so she let it pass. "It just surprised me. He really seemed to enjoy it."

"Of course he did. So what's he like, really?"

"He's...nice."

"Nice?" Layla could just see Stephanie's perfectly arched brows rising.

"Okay, he's smart, quick and has a sense of humor, too." All of which, she thought, she'd known before, simply from their phone conversations. "He...knows a lot of things, is interested in a lot of things."

"You sound surprised again," Stephanie said. "Don't tell me you're judging him by his looks?"

"It's just that I'd heard he was a workaholic of sorts," Layla said. "That sort of implies he doesn't have time for anything else."

That, she told herself, was why she had been surprised at the depth and breadth of his knowledge and interests. And she'd been incredibly moved by what he'd done when his parents had been killed; she sensed there was a great deal more to that story than his brief, almost curt words had betrayed.

"Everyone needs time for something else. Maybe somebody needs to change that for him," Stephanie said.

"Don't look at me," Layla said wryly.

She meant it. Even if things were different, she knew Ethan was more than she could deal with.

"Does that mean he didn't ask you out again?"

Bless Stephanie, she didn't see why he wouldn't. "He didn't ask me out this time," she reminded her.

"A technicality," Stephanie said dismissively.

"Steph, it wasn't a date. And no, he didn't ask me out. I never expected him to."

Wished, maybe. Fantasized, perhaps. But that silliness would remain forever her secret. She existed in the real world, and there were some givens in that world that wouldn't change. One of them was that she did not resemble the ideal woman. She had accepted that long ago, even if Stephanie hadn't.

She managed to divert her friend, and after making a date for lunch the next day, they hung up. For a while afterward Layla sat quietly, letting her mind wander as she sipped her wine.

Until Stephanie's words came back to her.

Don't tell me you're judging him by his looks?

Could it be true? Could that really have been part of her supposition? Of all people, could she have made that mistake? Could she have been as wrong in her assumptions about him as he had been about her?

She straightened in the chair and set her glass down on the side table. Chagrin filled her. In a strange way, she was as guilty as anyone of stereotyping. Guilty of what had so often been done to her.

She'd been fooled by his physical appearance into thinking he'd probably gone easily through life, sliding by on his looks. That he'd never had to work particularly hard because things just came more easily to the beautiful ones.

No one, she thought with a serious pang of guilt for her own lapse in judgment, who took on the care of two young girls at the age of seventeen had had it easy. That he'd even considered doing it told her worlds about him that he probably didn't even realize, and blasted the assumptions so many had that only women had the nurturing instinct, that it was always the woman who had to hold the family together. She wondered if he had any idea how remarkable he was.

An odd feeling, sad, wistful and vaguely familiar, filled her, catching her off guard and tightening her throat. For the first time in a very long time she wished things were different, that she could be different, could be not how she was, so that today could be real, could be just the first of many days like it.

The moment she recognized the old feeling she became angry at herself; she thought she'd left her image problems behind years ago. She was who and what she was; three days in the hospital and a furious lecture from her doctor had convinced her of that. Someday perhaps there would be a man who wouldn't care, but she sure wasn't going to put her life on hold until then. Life was for living, not waiting. Her life was full and, for the most part, happy, and she was content.

Ethan Winslow was merely a ripple. She might want him, but she didn't *need* him. Still, she would tuck away the memory of this day forever. It was worth saving, but only for what it had been, a beautiful, enjoyable day doing something she loved. The extra...esthetic value was just a bonus.

But she knew she would carry that sun-kissed image of him for a very long time.

Six

Ethan sat looking at his personal checkbook. It was a bit anemic at the moment; he'd gone out on a limb for the Collins project personally, putting a big chunk of his own money into the development program. He should be wincing at writing this check, but when he remembered Sunday and how completely relaxing and enjoyable it had been, he couldn't begrudge it.

He picked up his pen and began to fill out the top check. As he wrote, he began to think about that day again, as he had so many times over the past week. It struck him at odd moments, when the sun slanted through a window at a certain angle or struck a blond woman's hair, when he was in his car and caught a glimpse of the Pacific's jeweled facets glinting in the pure summer light, or when he heard someone laugh. And then he would smile. The feel of that day had stayed with him all week, only now, on Friday, beginning to fade.

He signed the check with a flourish.

The intercom on his phone buzzed. He tapped the button to activate it. "Yes?"

"You asked to be reminded of your lunch meeting with Mr. Oxford."

"Thanks, Karen. I'll be on my way in a minute."

He stood, picked up the leather portfolio that lay on his desk and checked it to be sure that the contracts were in it; his people had worked too hard on this sale for him to blow it by forgetting them. He grabbed his jacket off the back of his chair, where he persisted in putting it despite Karen's efforts to train him to use the hanger she carefully placed on the hook on the back of his office door.

He also picked up the check he'd just written; he would have Karen put it in an envelope and mail it off. He tossed his jacket over his shoulder and stepped out to his assistant's desk. Karen was on the phone, speaking rather intensely to someone. After a moment he realized it was probably her daughter, who was about to have her first child and was, as Karen had ruefully told him, a basket case about it. He lingered for a moment, the check in his hand.

And then he realized that his meeting with Oxford was barely two blocks away from the Alzheimer's Center. He hesitated. Karen kept talking into the receiver, and then he decided; he tucked the check into his pocket. He could easily drop it off on his way back after his meeting.

Odd, he thought later as he tucked the signed contracts back into his leather portfolio, he'd never found Art Oxford boring before, nor did he usually want to cut and run the moment the ink was dry on a deal—it was not only rude but bad business—but now it seemed the man would rattle on forever.

When the check for the meal finally came, he leaped at the break it gave him, implied he had another appointment, paid, and excused himself, thanking Oxford again before he went.

He pulled into the rear parking lot of the building, remembering that Layla's office was fairly close to the back door. He saw her car, the blue sport utility he'd seen at the marina, parked a couple of spaces away. He supposed he didn't have to give the check to her personally, but as long as he was here and she was here…

She was on the phone. She didn't notice him right away, so he was able to stand in the doorway and observe her for a moment. He didn't know if she was talking to a man on the other end, but if she was, he knew exactly how the guy felt. That voice was incredible.

He wondered what that man might be picturing, what he might imagine the woman with the voice would look like, and if he would be as wrong as Ethan had been. He felt a pang as he remembered the night of the auction and Layla's expression when she'd seen his reaction to her. A reaction she'd clearly seen enough times to recognize instantly.

She was wearing another of her tailored suits, this time in navy blue. He wondered if that choice was an effort to make her size fade away or a declaration that her body wasn't to be noticed. Her hair was back in its usual tidy, sleek twist, without even a loose strand to soften the look. Severe, he thought. Clothes and hair. As if she thought there was no reason to try to gild the lily.

Or as if she thought there was no lily to gild in the first place.

She looked up then and saw him, and he wasn't sure if her expression was one of surprise or shock. But after a second she merely smiled. A smile, he thought, that matched the voice—soft, warm, welcoming.

Her call ended, and she waved him in. "Hello," she said, and that voice made him take a deep breath.

He felt oddly twitchy and covered it by sitting in the chair in front of her desk. She didn't ask why he was there, and for a moment he'd forgotten why himself. "Hi," he finally said after a few seconds of awkward silence.

"Hi," she said back.

"I brought the check," he said, remembering at last and pulling it out of his pocket. She looked at the check for a moment before she took it, as if puzzled as to why he hadn't simply mailed it. "I was in the neighborhood," he said, wincing inwardly at how corny that sounded. It shouldn't bother him, he chided himself. After all, it wasn't as if he'd done it for any other reason, he couldn't help it if it sounded like a line.

"You don't have to do this, you know."

"I made a pledge." And your voice is still the sexiest thing I've ever heard, he added silently.

She hesitated for a moment longer before saying, "Then, thank you." She opened her middle desk drawer and slipped the check into a folder. "I'll get it to the treasurer."

He wasn't sure what else to say. Wasn't sure he wanted to say anything else. It looked as though the silence was going to stretch out again, but this time she broke it.

"Your evening with Gloria was last night, wasn't it? How did it go?"

He wondered if she remembered when everybody's date was and decided she probably did, or at least had the record of all of them someplace handy.

"Yes," he said, smiling. "It was fine. Fun. The museum is very nice. And Gloria has been to most of the places the exhibits are from. She's really something." ·

"Isn't she?" Layla said with a wide smile.

"I would just as soon have left after we saw the museum and spent the rest of the evening just having her tell me stories of her travels."

"She does have some marvelous ones. And she tells them so well."

"When she can stop talking about her two grandchildren," Ethan said, grinning to show it hadn't bothered him.

Layla laughed. "She is the proverbial doting grandmother, isn't she? It was sweet of you to listen."

He looked away then. He tried to bite back the thought that always came to him at times like this, but the words were out before he could.

"My niece will never know her grandparents. Maybe I appreciate them more than some people do."

He could feel her gaze on him and at last looked back at her. In her eyes he saw a quiet understanding. But again she didn't resort to the platitudes he'd come to expect. It was as though she knew he realized she understood, so she didn't find it necessary to dwell on what was a painful subject anyway. And he appreciated that all the more for its rarity.

"Any plans for children of your own?" she asked. "Or do you feel like you've already raised your kids?"

"In a way. And if I feel the need, there's my niece." He grinned. "Being an uncle is great. You take them out, rev them up and then hand 'em back to Mom."

Layla laughed. "You're the kind of uncle every kid would love to have."

"I try," he said with exaggerated modesty. "Gloria and I compared notes on where to take the little darlings to get them wide-eyed and wound up."

She laughed again, that great laugh that went with the voice. "You two," she said, "could be dangerous."

"Gloria's a dangerous kind of woman," he said. "I'll bet she kept her husband on his toes."

"She did."

"And I'll bet he loved every minute of it."

"Yes." Layla looked at him rather oddly.

Ethan lifted a brow at her. "What?"

"Nothing. I just...I'm glad you liked her."

"Why wouldn't I?"

"She's...too much for some people."

"Some men, you mean?"

Her mouth lifted at one corner. That lovely, full, kissable mouth. "Some. I think they sense she doesn't really need them to complete her, and that bothers them."

"And what about you, Layla?" he asked before he thought.

"I want to grow up to be just like her," she said.

Meaning what? Ethan wondered. That she didn't want or need a man, either? Or that she wasn't like that now, but wanted to be? Had she been hurt often enough that she no longer wanted to play that age-old game?

"No man in your life, then?" he asked.

"No."

No dissembling, no "not at the moment," no "not anymore." Just a simple no. No details, no extra information, nothing that told him if there had ever been a man in her life. He wanted to ask, except that she would probably tell him it was none of his business. Which, he supposed, was true. But he still wanted to know. Not for the usual reason a man wanted to know if a woman was involved with someone, of course. He might not be quite sure why he did want to know, but he was sure that wasn't the reason.

"Is that because you don't want one?" he finally asked.

Her eyes narrowed, and he knew he'd pushed too far. He'd made her angry, and he wasn't even sure why.

"I'll tell you what. I'll answer your question if you'll answer one of mine."

"What?" he asked, made wary by the look in her eyes, which were glinting green now.

"Who is it you don't want to see at The Oaks?"

Ethan sucked in a harsh breath. "Remind me not to step on your toes again. You go right for the exposed nerve, don't you?"

"I wasn't sure it was exposed. It was only a guess." She gave him a long, steady look. "Apparently it was a good guess. Who is it?"

He looked down at his hands, unable to hold her gaze.

"Was the story about your parents the truth?"

His head came up sharply. "What?"

"Was it true, or is it one of your parents who's at The Oaks?"

She thought he'd lied? About *that?* "No!"

"My apologies, then. But it's not unusual for people to be…unable to deal with the changes of Alzheimer's. To be embarrassed by those changes, afraid of them, unwilling to acknowledge that they have an afflicted family member. Or to be ashamed that they're unable to deal with it themselves any longer, that they've had to put a loved one in a place like The Oaks."

He wondered if he was paling with her every word; the chill was certainly growing as if he were. Everything she said was digging into a deeply buried, unhealed spot that had been raw for three years now.

"Who is it, Ethan?"

She had come around the desk without him even realizing it. She crouched beside his chair. The edge had vanished from her voice now; this was the soft, coaxing siren of a voice he'd once thought could lure a man anywhere.

He wasn't going to tell her. He didn't talk about this to anyone. Few people even knew—

"It's obviously someone very important to you. It's all right, Ethan. Sometimes there's no choice. Sometimes patients have to be in a place like The Oaks, for their own safety and physical well-being."

He looked at her then. "Absolution?"

"No. Just understanding."

"You kept your father at home."

"I told you, I was lucky. He didn't become violent. Didn't try to harm himself or anyone else. He didn't even wander much, and rarely became angry."

"Then how did you know he had it? Diagnosis is a questionable thing, isn't it?" He knew it was, knew that the only way a positive identification of the disease could be made was through an autopsy.

"Yes. The best we can do is generally eighty-five to ninety

percent accuracy in diagnosis.'' She shrugged. ''But I knew. He would do…silly things, like put on layers of heavy clothing on ninety-degree days. I started finding things in…odd places. His watch in the freezer, floppy disks in the toaster. The man had a command of English, French and Russian that was impeccable. Toward the end, he could barely communicate.''

''I'm sorry.'' It was inane, it was useless, but it was the only thing he could think of to say.

''Me, too. It's one of the worst, most insidious killers we have. It robs you of your mind first, and eventually your body.''

He let out a long, compressed breath. ''That's the nightmare. To lose your mind, slowly.''

She rested a hand on his knee, gently. That slight touch warmed him far more than it should have. He felt as though he owed her. After what she'd shared. But—

''It helps to talk,'' she said. ''To know you're not alone.''

Alone. God, he'd never felt so alone as the first time he'd walked into the office after that last trip to The Oaks.

''Who is it for you, Ethan?'' Her voice was soft, warm and irresistible.

''Pete Collins,'' he said at last. And once the name had escaped, the rest came tumbling out. ''The founder of W.C.T. He gave me a job when I needed one, even though I was only seventeen. It wasn't much salary-wise, but it was enough to keep us going. Then he gave me a raise and told me to quit my second job. He kept an eye on me as I moved up in the ranks. And later…he sort of took me under his wing.''

''Became your mentor?'' Layla asked.

''I guess that's what you'd call it. He started training me, teaching me. Then put me to work directly for him. Seven years ago, he made me a VP. He pushed me, hard. I thought it was just to make me prove myself to him, but later I realized…he was afraid he would run out of time.''

"He'd already been diagnosed?"

Ethan nodded. "He was having periods of confusion. And he was a man who was never, ever confused. And it made him furious. At himself."

"That's often the reaction."

"Once he found out, he started to plan. I didn't know it, I just thought he was still looking out for that scared kid he hired all those years ago."

"But he was grooming you to take his place."

Ethan nodded again. "He told me one day that he didn't have any children. And his only niece was in New York and would never leave there. I didn't realize...what he was telling me. Then."

"That you were going to be his heir."

"I never asked for it. If I'd known that's where he was headed..."

"You might have run?"

"I might have. I didn't think I was ready. But when the time came...there was no choice."

He leaned back in the chair. He felt battered, somehow, as if he'd been in some exhaustive conflict—and lost. He let his head loll back and his eyes close as he wondered how she'd managed to get him to pour out this sorry story.

Layla rose, leaning back against the edge of her battered, well-used desk. "When was the last time you saw him?"

His eyes snapped open; if he'd thought she was going to ease up now that he'd told her, he was obviously wrong.

"Come with me, Ethan."

For a moment he simply blinked, wondering just how she meant that. And then it registered what she must mean; she wanted him to come with her to The Oaks.

"No."

"Is he violent?"

"Sometimes. He gets very angry. He hides things and accuses the staff of stealing them. He tries to leave, then gets furious when he can't open the locked doors."

"Not unusual," she said. "Is he lucid at all?"

"Sometimes, for brief periods. But less and less all the time."

"Ethan, I know it's hard, but—"

"There's no point."

"No point?"

"The last time I was there, he didn't even know who I was."

She looked at him, long, steady and discomfiting. She turned and walked around her desk, and took her seat once more. "So," she said finally, "visiting is for you, not him?"

He blinked. "What?"

"You have to have his recognition to be there?"

He frowned. "To him I'm just…some stranger. My being there means nothing to him. They keep me posted on his condition, I see that he has whatever he needs, but there's nothing I can do for him."

She leaned back in her chair, her elbows on the worn arms as she steepled her fingers in front of her and looked at him consideringly. Her posture unsettled him, and he realized it was a position he often took himself.

"So you're of the opinion that he's better off with no visitors, left completely alone in what his life has become, than to have even someone he thinks is a stranger come see him?"

Ethan shifted uncomfortably. "I…" His voice trailed off; he'd never thought about it that way.

"You think he's better off thinking nobody cares about him anymore, rather than it be someone he doesn't quite remember?"

"No, but…"

"But it's hard? Of course it is. It's hard, it's painful and it's sometimes devastating to see someone you love, admire and respect reduced to a hollow shell. But if it's hard on you, imagine how it must be on him. During those periods of lucidity, when he knows what's happening, it must seem no one gives a damn.''

Ethan winced. Whatever else she was or wasn't, Layla Laraway clearly wasn't the kind to pull any punches.

''If Pete is as smart as he must be to have built your company, he probably knows, in those moments when he's functional, how bad it's getting. How little time he has left before that door in his mind slams shut forever.''

Ethan looked away from her. He wanted more than anything to get up out of this chair and leave, to put an end to this barrage of ugliness. But he couldn't seem to move.

''I knew one patient who had been a brilliant mathematician. He had no family, no close friends. After he was diagnosed, he did a calculation, some complex formula based on the duration of his 'outages,' as he called them, and the length of time between, by which he figured how much 'sane time' he had left. Then he picked a day.''

Ethan looked back at her then. ''A day?''

She nodded. ''The latest day of his life when he estimated he'd be rational enough to end it.''

Ethan stared. ''He picked a day to…kill himself?''

''He had his reasons. Some of them are hard to argue with.''

''Did he…do it?''

''No. The disease progressed faster than his formula had indicated. He's in the final stages now. But he's spent five years in the hell he wanted to avoid. Alone.''

Ethan sucked in a breath; it was impossible to miss her point, that Pete was in the same sinking ship. And that he was one of the deserting rats.

If she'd been trying to make him feel guilty, feel selfish, she'd succeeded. In fact, he felt like hell.

But he still didn't think he could face the ravaged shell of the man who had once been like a father to him.

He felt a wave of nausea roll through him.

He'd never realized before what a coward he was.

Seven

She'd been too rough on him, Layla thought glumly. She'd hit him with too much, too hard. Now not only wouldn't he go see his mentor, she would probably never see him again, either.

Not, she reminded herself, that she'd expected to see him again after their "date" anyway.

But he'd looked a little shell-shocked when he'd left her office Friday. She knew she sometimes got carried away by her passion about her cause, but she couldn't help feeling the way she did. Anytime she thought about slacking off or taking a break, memories of her father would come back to her. Of her father, with all his genius, reduced to a caricature of his former self, unable to find his way down a hallway, unable, finally, to simply count to ten because he couldn't hold the thought long enough. And then she went back to work with renewed vigor, even on Saturday evenings like this.

But that vigor was failing her at the moment. Almost a week ago she'd been sailing to Catalina. One day short of a week ago, she'd had one of the most perfect days of her life. And she was having trouble consigning it to the realm of once-in-a-lifetime occurrences, stuffing it into that mental box where she kept sweet memories that would be forever that, only memories.

She hadn't meant to scare Ethan off.

But had she? Had he come to her office for no other reason than what he'd said, to drop off the check since he was close by? She could hardly say she'd scared him off if he'd had no intention of returning or contacting her anyway.

And that, she told herself, was certainly that. She went back to work, finishing with the large stack of paperwork that had accumulated while she'd been so focused on coordinating the auction. It was only the routine things that remained, and she hoped to have those done today. She only wished the work itself was more of a challenge. It would keep her distracted from thoughts she shouldn't be having in the first place.

She didn't realize how unsuccessful she was being until her phone rang and, instead of her answering calmly, her heart began to race.

He doesn't even have your home phone number, idiot, she chastised herself as she reached for the receiver.

"Just checking in, girlfriend." Stephanie's voice was cheerful, as usual. "I was kind of hoping that you wouldn't be there."

"Where would I be?"

"Well, after that gorgeous Mr. Winslow came by your office yesterday, who knows?"

"He was there to drop off the check for his donation," Layla pointed out.

"He could have mailed it."

"Don't go reading anything into that, Stephanie."

"Why not? When a guy goes out of his way like that—"

"He was in the neighborhood. He had a meeting or something. Besides, his office is only a few blocks from mine. It's hardly out of his way to stop by.''

"Sure."

"Stephanie, don't be ridiculous."

"What's ridiculous?"

"The idea of him and…me."

"Why?"

Layla sighed. "I love you, Stephanie, but don't be obtuse. If you'd ever seen him, you'd know what I mean."

"But I have. I've seen photos of him, didn't I tell you? In an old news weekly, and in the paper the morning after the auction. He is most definitely fine. And prime."

"Exactly my point."

This time Stephanie sighed. "Layla, you've got to stop assuming no man will ever—"

"Stephanie, you've got to stop assuming it doesn't make any difference."

"I don't. I mean, I know it does. To some people. Maybe even to a lot of people. But darn it, not everyone. It never mattered to your father."

"That's because he never noticed."

Her father truly had never seemed to notice that first her mother, then Layla, was what was kindly called of regal size. But then, he was always so lost in his work that he rarely even noticed or cared how she looked; he was much more concerned about her brain than her body. He'd always told her she was smart, clever and kind, and therefore beautiful— because those were his standards of beauty—and it had been a rude shock to her when she realized just how different the rest of the world's standards were.

"Maybe Ethan doesn't, either. Or doesn't care."

Layla didn't want to admit how much she would love to believe that, so she tried a diversion. "You seem so interested, maybe you should go out with him."

"Uh-uh. You saw him first."

Layla chuckled. "That's you, dear old Stephanie, always

playing fair. Don't you know beautiful women are supposed to be shallow and ruthless?''

"Ha. My folks spent too much time teaching me how much harder I'd have to work to be taken seriously for me to buy into that.''

Layla knew it was true. Stephanie's mother was a psychologist and had made a point of seeing to it that her daughter learned her mind and her manner were more important than her looks. Growing up, she'd seen Stephanie's fledgling efforts at using her looks to manipulate squashed in the bud, and she had no doubt her friend was much the better for it.

But at least she'd managed to divert the conversation. And when they hung up, something lingered in Layla's mind: the idea that her beautiful, smart, sexy friend would be the perfect match for Ethan Winslow.

But first she had something to tell the man herself.

"Try it now.''

Ethan braced himself on the fender as Bill turned the key. This time, unlike the last three, the motor in the racy, expensive European coupe started.

"Hey, great! I knew I kept you around for a reason, buddy,'' Bill said as he got out of the driver's seat.

"I live to be useful,'' Ethan said from under the hood. Bill had absolutely no mechanical aptitude at all, so more than once Ethan had been drafted as mechanic to Bill's progressively more expensive string of cars. Before the accident that had ended Ethan's world as he knew it, when Bill had gotten his driver's license before Ethan could, they'd traded his work for rides; now it was for Bill's knack with computers. He had bailed out Ethan—whose expertise ended at knowing how to run his software—a few times, so he figured they were about even.

"If you wanted to be useful, you would have been here last Sunday, when it broke down. Where were you, anyway? We missed you for the game.''

"I was…sailing."

Bill's sandy brows rose. "Sailing?"

Ethan lifted his brows right back. "Yes. You know, a boat, lots of ropes, large pieces of canvas."

"Smart guy. What boat?"

"It belongs to a friend of…a friend."

"Who's this friend who has a friend with a boat you never told me about?"

Ethan sighed. "It was my auction date, all right?"

Bill gaped at him. "You went through with it?"

"Of course I did. I made a pledge."

"Yeah, I know all about you and promises. But…with the heifer?"

Ethan pulled back sharply, frowning. "You've never even met her."

"I saw her picture in the paper, after the auction. Now that's a *bi-iig* woman." He finished his dig with a rude, mooing sound.

Ethan's gut tightened. And so, he noticed peripherally, did his fists. He wanted to slug Bill for his tactlessness, his smugness and his cruelty. And most of all for the carelessness of it, as if it didn't matter.

"Shut up," he snapped.

Bill looked startled. "Hey, I only said what any guy—"

"I heard what you said. And you're out of line. She's a…nice woman, and she doesn't deserve that."

Bill at least had the grace to look abashed. "Okay, okay, she's nice. I guess she'd have to be."

Ethan resisted reaching for the wrench he'd just been using and braining Bill, but it wasn't easy. And yet he knew Bill's view was common. Too common. To be brutally honest, he supposed he'd thought something similar on occasion himself. Not as crudely, true, but he wasn't sure that ameliorated it much.

And Layla had to deal with this every day.

"What's with you?"

"I wish I knew," Ethan muttered to himself.

But he did know. It was simply that what he'd said was true, Layla was a nice woman, and she didn't deserve to be bad-mouthed, especially by someone who'd never even spoken to her.

Bill looked nothing more than puzzled. He really didn't get it, Ethan thought as he watched his friend lean over to close the hood on the silver coupe. Something caught his eye, and without much forethought, he spoke.

"Getting really thin there on top, eh, buddy?"

Bill straightened sharply. "What?"

"You're gonna be needing spray paint to cover that bald spot soon."

Bill flushed; he was very sensitive about his thinning hair, and among his friends it was generally off-limits to even good-natured teasing.

"Better grab one of those supermodels while you can, they don't hang with bald guys."

Bill swore, his face even redder, and he looked as if he wanted to take a swing.

"Don't like it, do you?" Ethan said. "Think about it."

Bill was too aggravated to think right now, Ethan knew, but maybe later… Maybe later he would realize that he shouldn't be dishing it out if he couldn't take it.

Maybe.

Layla glanced up to double check the address, although she knew she hadn't made a mistake. She stepped thankfully inside the air-conditioned lobby of the office building. It was surprisingly cheerful despite an excess of cold glass and metal; someone had chosen brightly colored pieces of textured art to place on the walls, and the elevator doors were a bright blue that matched the sky outside.

W.C.T. occupied, she saw from the building directory, several floors, starting on the third. She couldn't resist looking farther and found not Ethan's name, but that of Peter Collins, still listed under the executive offices on the fifth floor. She wondered if it was an oversight or intentional that it hadn't been changed, even after all this time. She suspected that, on Ethan's part, at least, it was intentional.

A man got on the elevator behind her, pressed a button, then stepped to one side. She felt his glance, but it didn't linger, nor did he speak. Or even smile. She was part of the surroundings, nothing more, a true wallflower.

She shouldn't feel anything, she told herself. She worked rather hard at blending in with the background, at making sure nothing she did or wore called any attention to her. Trying to make her size fade into the woodwork. She was successful enough, she supposed; no one seemed to notice her much. She wasn't morbidly obese, so didn't draw shocked stares or, fortunately, snickers. And since she wasn't the size eight or smaller that seemed to be required for the other kind of attention, she didn't get that, either. So she blended, was looked past, not at, and was happy enough about it.

And Stephanie telling her that she was seeing things through a cockeyed filter, that she was hiding her light under a bushel, wasn't going to change that.

The elevator door slid open smoothly on the fifth floor. She stepped into a small reception area that was as bright and cheerful as the downstairs lobby had been. And as her own living room was, she thought in sudden realization, with many of the same colors.

There was a reception counter to her right, but what caught her eye was the large—at least eight feet long, she thought—saltwater aquarium. It was full of brilliantly colored tropical fish, and she knew where the decorator had come up with the color palette for the office. It made her smile, this touch of lovely, living whimsy in the offices of what most would assume would be a cold, technically fixated place.

There was a young man behind the counter and a young woman on this side, and they were chatting easily, obviously

quite familiar with each other. Layla walked to the counter,
the envelope she'd come to deliver in her hand, her eyes on
a darting fish in the tank, one so yellow he seemed to glow
in the crystal-clear water.

The conversation stopped the moment she arrived. She
glanced at the two. The chat had clearly been personal, so
she supposed they were putting it on hold to attend to business, meaning her.

"This will be quick," she promised with a smile at them
both. "I just wanted to drop this off for Mr. Winslow."

The young woman, attractive in a casual but stylish peach-
colored sweater and slacks that went well with her blue eyes
and dark hair, looked at her. She reminded Layla of someone,
but before she could place the resemblance, the young man
spoke.

"Of course. Did you need to see him?"

"No," she said hastily. "If you could just see that he gets
it? No rush, it's…personal."

"Certainly." He took the envelope from her just as the
phone at his elbow rang, and with a quick "Excuse me," he
answered it.

Layla began to turn away, but the woman beside her
stopped her with a word.

"Personal?" she said.

Startled by the seeming rudeness of the inquiry, Layla said
rather coolly, "Yes," and stepped back, preparing to leave.

The woman smiled, rather sheepishly. "I'm sorry. You
must think I'm a real buttinsky. But you see, Ethan's my
brother. I just came from his office."

Instantly, Layla's annoyance vanished and a smile curved
her mouth. "You must be Sarah," she said.

The woman brightened noticeably. "He told you about
me?"

"Yes. I assumed it must be you, since he said your sister's
up in Orange."

She seemed disproportionately delighted at that. Her hair

slid back as she looked up at Layla, revealing a series of three gold rings marching down the outside rim of her left ear, ending with a dangling star at her earlobe. "He told you about her, too?"

"Margaret-don't-ever-call-me-Maggie? Yes, he did."

Sarah laughed. It was like her brother's laugh, light and infectious. She leaned back against the counter as if she were settling in for a long chat.

"He must like you, then. I don't think he claims us to just anyone."

Layla laughed in turn. "On the contrary. He's quite proud of you both."

"Well, Margaret, maybe. I'm just a thorn in his side most of the time."

Layla belatedly realized she hadn't introduced herself. "I'm Layla Laraway," she said, holding out her hand.

Sarah took it, her eyes lighting up again. "The auction!" she exclaimed, looking at Layla assessingly.

"Afraid so," Layla said ruefully.

Apparently reading Layla's tone, Sarah said quickly, "No, really, Ethan had a wonderful time. He used to love to sail, but he never takes time for it—or anything else—anymore. I was so glad you got him to go."

"He seemed to enjoy it," Layla said carefully.

"Oh, he did. I saw him that evening, and he hasn't been that relaxed in a long time. I've been hoping to meet you, to thank you for that. And," she added with a sly grin, "to find out how you got him to agree to that auction in the first place."

Sarah's artless, openhearted manner was irresistible. "Looking for lessons?"

Sarah laughed again. "Oh, no wonder he had fun. Come, talk to me," she said, urging Layla to take a seat in the waiting area. "Can you get him to go again? He's turning into a first-class workaholic."

"Is he?"

"It's my fault, of course. Mine and Margaret's." Her voice was still light, but Layla sensed a note of frankness in the words; Sarah really believed this.

"What do you mean?"

Sarah looked at her consideringly. "Did he tell you? About us? The family, I mean?"

"About your parents? Yes. It must have been so awful for you."

Sarah seemed to assess that, whether it was Layla's words or that her brother had revealed this to her, as well, Layla couldn't tell. After a moment Sarah acknowledged the reality simply, with sincerity but without moroseness.

"It was. We were hurting so bad, and we were so young. We didn't realize that Ethan was driving himself into the ground for us."

"Oh?" She was immensely curious, Layla realized, and didn't want Ethan's sister to stop now.

Sarah nodded. "He fought like crazy to keep us together, when the powers that be seemed set on splitting us up, sending us all to different foster homes. He was only seventeen, but he fought like…like our father would have."

Layla felt a sudden tightness in her throat. She'd known it couldn't have been as easy as he'd made it sound.

"Margaret was twelve when they were killed, I was only ten. But Ethan refused to believe it wasn't for the best that we stay together. He worked two jobs to provide for us, and went to college at night to hang on to our parents' dream for him. If he got more than two or three hours of sleep a night for five years, I'd be surprised."

"Lord," Layla murmured. She'd known Ethan was something special, but this…

"Yes," Sarah agreed. "And not only that, his social life was dead. Not many girls were interested in a guy his age who came with two little sisters as part of the package. But he never held it against us, never made us feel like we were…ruining his life."

"No," Layla said softly. "He wouldn't."

"He taught us everything that really matters. To work hard at whatever we do, to take care of each other, to take a stand, to be honest. We didn't appreciate it then. Or him. At least, not enough."

"Children often don't. It takes some growing up, something to compare it to, to understand a sacrifice like that. And to treasure it properly."

"We do—now. I don't think he knows just how much, though. I keep trying to tell him, but he's such a guy, he just shrugs and says 'Yeah, yeah.'"

Layla smiled. "I can picture that perfectly."

"You know, a lot of people wrote him off as just a pretty face when he was a kid."

Layla's mouth twisted. "He's not exactly ugly now."

Sarah grinned. "No, he's not, is he?" She sighed dramatically. "You have no idea how horrible it is to have such a hunky brother. Girls swooning right and left. It gets so awfully messy."

Layla laughed, she couldn't help it, but behind the outward amusement there was a twinge of something darker, painful, as the reality of Ethan Winslow's options was brought home once more. He could pick and choose, and when he got around to it, he no doubt would.

"But you know what they do wrong?" Sarah asked.

"Er…who?" Layla had to ask; she'd momentarily lost the thread.

"Those girls. They just don't understand him at all. They take one look at him and figure he's some slick, smooth, dashing type, who'll take them out to exotic places for gourmet dinners and the best champagne. Not that he wouldn't, he's not stingy or anything," Sarah hastened to add. "He's always spending money on us."

"But?" Layla asked, undeniably curious again; she was getting a very personal glimpse into the man who had her so fascinated, and she wasn't, she admitted to her chagrin, above wanting more.

"I mean, he looks like a race car driver, or an actor, or something glamorous or dangerous, but inside he's a guy who likes dinner at home, or a walk in the rain, or a picnic in some mountain meadow or something."

The outside didn't match the inside, Layla thought. Here was proof that she had indeed been as wrong about him as others were about her. That she, too, had made assumptions based on looks. She didn't like having it done to her, and here she'd done it to him, with barely a second thought.

She left the W.C.T. building, Sarah's pleas that she get Ethan out on the water again soon still echoing in her ears, and walked slowly back to her Blazer, thinking.

She had, it seemed, a bit left to learn about looks and perceptions and stereotypes herself.

Eight

"Here's your mail, sir. If that's all, I'm off to my luncheon."

Ethan looked up at Karen as she set a small stack of envelopes on his desk. When he'd first taken over, he'd tried for months to break her of the "sir" habit, but it had been a wasted effort.

"Have a good time," he said; her annual sorority reunion luncheon was one of the few times Karen ever asked for extra time, and he was happy to okay it.

"What will you be doing for lunch?"

He smiled. "Don't worry about me. I'll eat something."

She sniffed. "Some fast-food thing, I'm sure."

"Maybe," he said with a laugh. "I'm just enjoying the novelty of not having a lunch meeting."

"Try a personal lunch for a change," she said as she turned and left.

A personal lunch. Now there was a concept. He leaned

back in his chair, tapping his pen against his index finger. Problem was, with whom? Who would be available on no notice on a business Monday?

"Damn," Ethan muttered. This was pretty sad. Except for his sisters, he couldn't think of one single person he knew well enough to ask to lunch who didn't have something to do with work. Except Bill, and he'd had about enough of him for the moment, with his comments about Layla.

Layla. Now there was someone not connected to work.

He stopped tapping his pen. How could he even consider that, after the way they'd parted? She'd blasted him almost to bits with her merciless passion, then left him sitting in her office, still reeling, while she left to do what he lacked the courage for.

He tossed his pen down on the desk and reached for the mail, desperate for a distraction. Whether from thoughts of the woman who so disturbed him or the reminder of the major failing in his life, he wasn't sure.

As usual, the efficient Karen had sorted them, labeling the outside of each envelope with an appropriate reference to whatever it was regarding. He set aside two that he knew were invitations to annual social events—summer was a hot time in this town in more ways than one—tossed one he knew was an advertisement into his wastebasket, and left a thick one with a University of California return address in front of him to look at before the day was out; the man was consulting on the Collins project, and this must be the research paper he'd promised.

The next one stopped him dead.

He'd seen the writing before, on a well-used clipboard at the auction, on notes left on a desk. It was distinctive, a bold, slashing script that was almost art in itself.

Layla Laraway.

The return address wasn't her office, but he still knew it was her. And it wasn't an official envelope, but a personal one, pale blue. He picked it up, tapped it against the blotter on his desk and, finally, opened it.

It was short. His name, followed by only three lines.

I get carried away. You didn't need to hear all of that at once. I'm sorry.

Her signature was as bold and self-assured as the rest of the writing. And he smiled as he realized she hadn't said he didn't need to hear what she'd said, only that he hadn't needed to hear it all at once. She might apologize for how she'd presented them, but she wouldn't compromise her beliefs. Funny, how he was so certain of that. He shouldn't be, given the short time he'd known her. But he was.

But she had apologized, and graciously. She didn't have to. Many wouldn't have, but she had.

He folded the note and slipped it back into the envelope. And noticed for the first time that it had no stamp. It must have been hand delivered.

He frowned, wondering why she hadn't come to his office if she'd been in the building. Did she think he wouldn't accept her apology? Or had it been something else that had made her avoid seeing him? He tapped the envelope on his desk blotter a couple more times. He reached for the telephone, then stopped.

Maybe he should just drop in, see what she was doing. That way, if it was obvious she was too busy for lunch, he wouldn't have to ask. Her office was close, barely a few blocks away; it wouldn't be a hassle to go by.

It seemed like such a good idea that he was on his feet and moving before he thought much more about it. And even when he did, it still seemed like a good idea; her note of apology needed some kind of response, and lunch seemed a nice way to say "apology accepted."

He grabbed his jacket, didn't bother with the tie he'd discarded earlier that morning and headed out the door. He took a back route that kept him off the main drag and out of the typical lunchtime traffic, and was at Layla's office in minutes.

It was busier this time than it had been on Friday. There were people bustling around, and others sitting and waiting...for what, he didn't know. The receptionist smiled, seeming to recognize him from his earlier visit.

"Are you looking for Layla?"

He nodded. He wasn't sure how he felt about the assumption, then told himself it was only natural; she'd been his only real contact with the organization, after all.

"Down that hall," the young man said, gesturing in the opposite direction from where Ethan knew her office was located. "Second door on the right."

Ethan nodded, murmured a thank-you, and started that way. He hesitated when he saw the door that had been indicated was labeled Testing, but it was propped open, so he stepped inside.

The room was empty. There were two other doorways on the far wall, and one of those stood open. He headed toward it, and by the time he was a yard away, he could see Layla standing beyond it, in a small room with a table, four chairs and what seemed to be an abnormally large window. She was facing that window, looking intently at something.

She saw him, held a finger to her lips for quiet, but gestured him inside. He stepped into the room and immediately wanted to back right out again. The moment he saw what they were doing on the other side of what was apparently a one-way mirror, he realized what the word "testing" on the door had meant.

The poor soul in that room, a grandmotherly lady wearing a single strand of pearls, was about to have the rest of her life taken away. He could feel it, that she was about to be told it was all downhill from here, that she could expect nothing but to get worse, to gradually lose all cognitive function, and there was not a damned thing anyone could do to stop it.

He stared into the room, mesmerized the way people were when passing a messy wreck on a highway.

God, what they're doing to you...

He must have said some part of it, because Layla looked at him and spoke as if he'd asked the logical question.

"It's the M.M.S.E.," she said softly. "The Mini Mental Status Examination."

He looked at her, which was much more pleasant than looking at what was happening in the testing room. "It's really called that?"

She nodded. "It's come into widespread use as an initial test when some form of dementia is suspected."

The older woman neatly folded a piece of paper, bent over and placed it on the floor.

"What did she ask her to do, make a paper airplane?" He knew he sounded bitter, but he couldn't help himself, not when he remembered how Pete, a man who had run a sizable corporation, had been unable to follow the simplest of commands.

"No," Layla said, not reacting to his tone, "she asked her to do exactly what she did. In fact, she's doing quite well. She's going to be close to thirty points, and we only recommend additional testing at twenty-five or worse."

He looked back at the woman then, who was writing something down for the tester.

"She's asking for a sentence with a subject and a verb."

Ethan watched the woman as she finished and set down the pencil. The examiner picked up what she'd written, and a smile flashed across her face. Her eyes flicked to the mirror, and Ethan instinctively backed up a step. But this was obviously for Layla, who smiled widely as the examiner read, "The sometimes forgetful old woman passed the test."

"She's just fine," Layla said, chuckling now.

"Then why is she here?"

"She was concerned about her absentmindedness, afraid it was something more serious."

"But it's not?"

"Not yet, anyway." As the two women in the other room

How To Play:

No Risk!

1. With a coin, carefully scratch off the 3 gold areas on your Lucky Carnival Wheel. By doing so you have qualified to receive everything revealed — 2 FREE books and a surprise gift — ABSOLUTELY FREE!

2. Send back this card and you'll receive brand-new Silhouette Desire® novels. These books have a cover price of $3.99 each in the U.S. and $4.50 each in Canada, but they are yours TOTALLY FREE!

3. There's no catch! You're under no obligation to buy anything. We charge nothing — ZERO — for your first shipment. And you don't have to make any minimum number of purchases — not even one!

4. The fact is thousands of readers enjoy receiving books by mail from the Silhouette Reader Service™. They enjoy the convenience of home delivery…they like getting the best new novels at discount prices, BEFORE they're available in stores…and they love their *Heart to Heart* subscriber newsletter featuring author news, horoscopes, recipes, book reviews and much more!

5. We hope that after receiving your free books you'll want to remain a subscriber. But the choice is yours — to continue or cancel, anytime at all! So why not take us up on our invitation, with no risk of any kind. You'll be glad you did.

No Cost!

LUCKY
Carnival Wheel

Find Out Instantly The Gifts You Get Absolutely FREE!

Scratch-off Game →

LOSER — WINNER — WINNER — LOSER — WINNER

LUCKY CARNIVAL WHEEL

YES!

I have scratched off the 3 Gold Areas above. Please send me the 2 FREE books and gift for which I qualify! I understand I am under no obligation to purchase any books, as explained on the back and on the opposite page.

326 SDL CY4L   **225 SDL CY4G**

NAME   (PLEASE PRINT CLEARLY)

ADDRESS

APT.#   CITY

STATE/PROV.   ZIP/POSTAL CODE

The Silhouette Reader Service™ — Here's how it works:

Accepting your 2 free books and gift places you under no obligation to buy anything. You may keep the books and gift and return the shipping statement marked "cancel." If you do not cancel, about a month later we'll send you 6 additional novels and bill you just $3.34 each in the U.S., or $3.74 each in Canada, plus 25¢ delivery per book and applicable taxes if any.* That's the complete price and — compared to cover prices of $3.99 each in the U.S. and $4.50 each in Canada — it's quite a bargain! You may cancel at any time, but if you choose to continue, every month we'll send you 6 more books, which you may either purchase at the discount price or return to us and cancel your subscription.

*Terms and prices subject to change without notice. Sales tax applicable in N.Y. Canadian residents will be charged applicable provincial taxes and GST.

If offer card is missing write to: Silhouette Reader Service, 3010 Walden Ave., P.O. Box 1867, Buffalo, NY 14240-1867

BUSINESS REPLY MAIL
FIRST-CLASS MAIL   PERMIT NO. 717   BUFFALO, NY

POSTAGE WILL BE PAID BY ADDRESSEE

SILHOUETTE READER SERVICE
3010 WALDEN AVE
PO BOX 1867
BUFFALO NY 14240-9952

NO POSTAGE
NECESSARY
IF MAILED
IN THE
UNITED STATES

rose and started toward the door, Layla gave him a sideways look. "There's a lot of truth in the old layman's diagnosis that if you forget where you put your keys, you're absent-minded, but if you forget what keys do, it's Alzheimer's."

"So what happens now?"

"We have some memory assistance classes we can refer her to, which most people find helpful. We'll start with that."

"What if she'd failed the test?"

"One failure isn't a diagnosis. If it continues, there are additional tests. And physical or organic causes have to be eliminated, and there are a lot of them. If necessary, if the symptoms persist and a diagnosis is still questionable, a CT or even a PET scan can eliminate the last possibilities of another cause."

She knew her stuff, Ethan thought. She cared, a great deal, that was obvious. But it didn't make the result any more palatable.

"Diagnosis as a process of elimination," he muttered.

"Unfortunately, yes. But the only positive diagnosis is—"

"I know. An autopsy." Bitterness soured his voice. "Wonderful."

She turned to face him. "I hate this damned disease just as much as you do, you know. I loathe it, and what it does, what it steals."

She didn't go on as they stepped out into the hall, but Ethan could hear the words, "But I choose to do something about it" as clearly as if she had spoken them. But there wasn't a trace of condemnation in her eyes, or of chastisement in her voice, so perhaps it was his own subconscious—or his conscience—providing the words. The lingering after-effect of the guilt that had swamped him on Friday, in her office, when she'd made him feel like such a coward.

She'd also awed him with her passion, the same passion that fairly shimmered in her now. And he wondered what else in her life she cared about as much as this, what else she felt as deeply. If anything.

They passed an elderly couple as they walked. The man was leaning heavily on a woman who looked too frail to support him, but she was doing it just the same.

"Hello, Mr. and Mrs. Kaplan," Layla said.

"Hello, Layla," the woman said.

The man just looked at Layla and frowned. "Why are you dressed like that, Sophy? What happened to those pretty dresses I bought you?"

Mrs. Kaplan's face contorted, and Ethan saw her blink rapidly.

Layla put a gentle hand on the weary woman's shoulder and smiled at the man. "I'll wear one of them tomorrow," Layla said gently. "Just for you."

The man smiled back. "That's my girl."

Layla turned warm, compassionate eyes on the woman. "The aide will be out tomorrow, Mrs. Kaplan. Will you be all right until then?"

"We'll be fine. Bless you, child."

Ethan watched them go. Then he looked back at Layla. "Who's Sophy?"

"Their daughter. She drowned twenty years ago."

Ethan winced inwardly. "Do you...look like her?"

"Not at all."

"Does he always think you're her?"

She shook her head. "No. Sometimes he knows exactly who I am." She sighed. "It's the day he doesn't recognize Ethel, after forty-two years of marriage, that will be the toughest. But it hasn't come yet."

The thought—indeed, the entire encounter—had unsettled him. How did people deal with it? How did she? She truly did care. This gentle concern and compassion was no act. She hated the enemy but never lost sight of the victims.

He wondered why he was finding it so hard to simply do what he'd come for, invite her to lunch. They walked on, passing a few more people on the way to her office. All of them smiled widely and greeted her warmly, with no pretense that he could see. Layla's assistant was at his desk, but most of those he'd seen when he'd come in weren't in sight now. Gone to lunch, he imagined, chiding himself to get on with it.

When he finally managed it, just as they reached her office, she looked surprised. "You could just say you accept my apology, you know."

"I plan to," he said. "Over lunch."

She hesitated. "I have a lot to do here—"

"Go to lunch!" Her assistant must have heard them, Ethan realized. And he wasn't the least bit embarrassed at eavesdropping, judging by the smile on the young man's face. "She works too hard," he told Ethan. "We all know it, but we can't get her to take a break. So if you can, please, please do."

A world of fondness and respect was in his voice; Layla was clearly held in considerable esteem around here. Not that that surprised him. From everything he'd seen, she deserved every bit of it.

"I'm trying," he quipped. "If she'll just let me."

Layla blushed, rather charmingly, he thought. "All right," she said at last.

He wished she hadn't sounded quite so pressured about it.

"I met your sister this morning," Layla said as their food arrived.

Ethan's brows furrowed, but after a split second he said, "At my office? When you dropped off the note?"

He'd put that together quickly, she thought. "She's charming."

"She can be," he admitted.

"She also said she was periodically a thorn in your side."

"She can be that, too," he agreed ruefully.

They both tried their sandwiches, agreed they were good, and ate for a minute or two in silence. Then, as she reached for the diet soda she drank for the taste, not the lack of calories, she went on.

"Sarah loves you very much."

"We're pretty close. We had to be."

"She's afraid you don't know how much she and her sister appreciate what you did to keep you all together."

"You had quite a talk, I see," he said wryly. Then he shrugged, just as Sarah had predicted. "It had to be done."

Layla wondered how many miracles had been born of men who simply said "It had to be done" and then went ahead and did it. She didn't have to wonder what he would say if she broached that fanciful thought; he would brush it off as absurd. In his mind, he'd done just that: only what had to be done. Nothing special, nothing grand. Never seeing how special that in itself was.

Another boy in the same position might have abandoned his sisters, lacking the bond, the drive, the responsibility or the confidence, to even consider taking on such a burden. But Ethan had had all of those qualities. He must have, or he wouldn't have pulled it off, and done it so well; from everything she'd seen and heard, Sarah and Margaret were testimony to his success.

No, Ethan Winslow would never abandon those he loved. He wouldn't—

She stopped her own thoughts as another realization struck. It *wasn't* in his nature to abandon someone he cared about. And yet he had, for all intents and purposes, abandoned Peter Collins.

She considered that thoughtfully as they continued their meal. That would explain the tension, the hostility she'd come up against when she'd brought up going to The Oaks to him. She'd guessed he felt guilty about not seeing his mentor, but now she thought she understood why he'd reacted so powerfully. It was totally against his nature, and he was torn by the battle.

"And where did you slip off to?" he asked her.

"I was just thinking. About…your mentor."

He went very still. "I'd rather not discuss that."

"I know," she said gently. "And I think I understand now. It must have been like…losing another parent. And you'd already been through that, losing both your mother and father."

He didn't answer, but she saw his hand tighten around his glass until the knuckles whitened. He'd been through so much pain in his life, starting at an age when he should have been thinking about cars and proms and a golden future. He'd been so strong for two little girls; what right did anyone have to ask him to go through a different agony all over again? Or to blame him for pretending it wasn't happening, if that was the only way he could stand it?

"I truly am sorry I…pushed you like I did. We all have to deal with losses like this in our own way, whether it's to uselessly fight a battle whose result is decided before you begin, or to pull back to where you can stand the pain. I can't tell you how to deal with your own situation."

"But you think I should go see him."

"I think it's not my decision. And I have no right to judge you for whatever decision you make. You're already doing more than most people, with your donations and, especially, with the Collins project. You have no reason to feel guilty."

She meant it; they'd talked about the project, and if he succeeded, it would be the kind of miracle they all prayed for. And if his quiet, stubborn determination was anything to judge by, someday he *would* succeed.

To her relief, he let it pass. And when the waitress came to check on them, he seemed back to his usual, cheerful self.

She probably, however, would not be getting any more lunch invitations, Layla thought somewhat glumly.

But that, she told herself, would be just as well.

Nine

This had to stop.

Layla had never been given to fidgeting, but she was learning fast. She'd never been so relentlessly restless as she had been in the past few weeks. Not that she didn't have reason.

She'd been wrong. Quite wrong. At least once a week, more often two or three times, she'd gotten a phone call from Ethan Winslow asking if she was free for lunch. For three straight weeks. And each time, over the fierce protestations of her own common sense, she'd said yes.

It wasn't that she didn't enjoy every minute of the time she spent with him. Well, every minute other than those spent noticing the sidelong glances she got wherever they happened to be.

For all they know, she told herself, it's a business lunch.

There certainly wasn't anything going on that would indicate otherwise. They didn't flirt or touch or walk out holding hands, nothing that would make anyone think they were on a date. Because they weren't dates, they were just...lunch.

No one could really be thinking they were anything more than casual acquaintances. Or maybe relatives. They could be thinking he was her brother or something.

She determined that that was how she would look at it from now on, however long it lasted. It would be the smartest thing she could do. She knew that.

She also knew it was impossible.

But no one else had to know that. Most especially Ethan. He would probably be completely embarrassed if he knew which way her thoughts were wandering. As would she, if he ever found out. So she would make sure he didn't.

She would enjoy these encounters for what they were and stop projecting her feelings onto them, stop wishing they could be more than they were.

Too bad it was so much easier said than done.

Just relax and be yourself. You're smart, you're exceptionally witty, and whether you believe it or not, you're lovely.

Stephanie's words, so often spoken, rang in her head, but they didn't help much. Stephanie wouldn't be in these straits. She would be comfortable seeing any man's undivided attention as her due, simply because she'd never done without it.

"—million miles away."

She suddenly focused across the table on Ethan, realizing he'd been talking and she'd been...fighting old battles. Rather impulsively she said, "I'm sorry. I was just thinking about...uh, Stephanie."

"Your friend whose family owns the boat?"

She nodded, surprised, and pleased, that he remembered. "You should meet her," she said. "I think you would get along. You have a lot in common." *You're both gorgeous,* she added silently.

"Oh?"

Layla considered his tone. He seemed receptive. Certainly more than Stephanie had been. So she reached into her purse and pulled out her organizer, opened it to the photo she carried and held it out to him.

It was of herself and Stephanie aboard the *Willow*, drenched in sun and tousled by the wind, and to her mind it captured the essence of her friend, alive, beautiful, joyous, happy.

"Looks like it was a fun day."

"It was. Isn't she beautiful?" she asked, curious that he hadn't commented as most men did.

"Looks that way," he said.

"I could introduce you," she suggested. "I...she's not serious about anyone right now."

Ethan, who had been lifting his glass for a drink, stopped with it midway to his mouth. He looked at her over the rim for a long, silent moment that made her wonder what he was thinking. He seemed to be thinking intently, assessing, and she wondered if by some chance he saw through what she'd been trying to do.

"Worried about my social life?" he finally asked, completely ignoring her hint. "You should talk to Sarah. She's convinced I'm trying out for the priesthood."

His tone was wry, but loving, and she decided she liked Sarah even more for having the nerve to tell him that. But it still surprised her; she couldn't imagine him doing without companionship. Unless he wanted it that way.

Which perhaps he did, Layla thought later when she was back in her office and pondering the situation. Maybe that was why he'd ignored her offer. The offer she wasn't sure why she'd even made.

What she'd said was true. She thought Ethan and Stephanie did have a lot in common, and that they would get along. That had to be why she'd done it. And it wasn't as though she and Ethan were...involved. She'd thought of it because she thought he and her friend would be a good couple.

Or because she was a coward, she told herself glumly. She could far too easily fall for the man, and that would be the kind of folly she'd left behind in Wayne's wake. It would be much easier on her if she matched him up with someone like Stephanie, someone who would keep him entranced and busy so that she could get on with her quiet, calm life.

That that life—which had always seemed so full with her work and friends—was beginning to feel a bit empty was her problem.

"I just don't get you, buddy. You could have any woman in town—hell, in half the state—with a snap of your fingers, but…" Bill hesitated, and Ethan guessed he was remembering the last time he'd insulted Layla. "That one?" he ended rather lamely. "I mean, I know you said she had the sexiest voice in town, but jeez, Ethan, she sure doesn't match it."

Odd, Ethan thought. He hadn't thought of her voice in that way for a while now. It was simply part of her, not some disembodied voice that raised the blood pressure. It was Layla's voice, not a voice that she didn't match.

"I can't believe you're still seeing her," Bill yammered on. "Especially if she tried to set you up with some hot, gorgeous friend of hers."

"It's only lunch now and then," Ethan said, feeling a bit defensive, and wishing he'd never mentioned Layla trying to set him up with her friend. He'd never realized before just how much his friend focused on looks.

"Just lunch? Oh." Bill shrugged. "Okay."

Okay? He'd been close to suggesting Ethan be locked away, but now it was okay? Just because it was only lunch?

The shrill chirp of a beeper distracted them both. Bill determined it was his and got up to go to the phone in the back of the coffee shop. It wasn't their usual kind of get-together, but Bill was heading out of town for the weekend, and Ethan had agreed to keep an eye on his place and feed his small collection of tropical fish, and he'd needed a key.

Ethan stirred his coffee, watching the dark liquid swirl. This was the first time he'd seen Bill since the day he'd called him on his harsh words about Layla. Bill had caught himself this time, but somehow Ethan didn't feel much better. His friend's obvious relief when he'd learned that Ethan's meetings with Layla had been only lunches nettled him.

Had he done the same himself? Had he subconsciously kept their encounters to lunches so that no one would think it was anything beyond friendship? Was he, in his own way, as bad as Bill was?

He didn't like the feeling. But at the same time, he didn't know if he wanted it to be anything more than friendship, so what was wrong with just lunch?

And that left him wondering why he wasn't sure. He liked her. He liked her wit, her caring, her ability to laugh so easily, her gentleness, her compassion, her generosity....

Okay, there was a long list of reasons for. So what was against? What was holding him back?

He could only think of one, a single reason why he hadn't pursued changing this relationship into something more personal. And he didn't like the reason. It made him feel vaguely uncomfortable, as if he'd discovered his own lack of depth while he'd been criticizing his friend for his shallowness.

It wasn't that he didn't think she was attractive, in her own way. She had incredible eyes, her hair was a beautiful, natural shade of blond—he'd caught himself wondering more than once how long it was and how it would look down, out of the omnipresent twist.

And that mouth of hers...

But there was no way around the fact that she wasn't the current ideal of female figures. And he knew she knew that. Maybe that was why she'd tried to set him up with—

"Ethan Winslow?"

He snapped out of his uncomfortable reverie and looked up at the woman who had stopped beside the table. Instinctively he got to his feet. "I...yes."

She was stunning. Petite, dark hair, short and gleaming, exotically tilted dark eyes, and a body that was the stuff of magazine covers and film close-ups. Of all the things he usually was drawn to in a woman, she had most of them.

And he knew her. Or, at least, he recognized her.

"You're...Stephanie? Layla's friend?"

The woman smiled, and it was a gut-tightener. "I didn't think you'd know me."

"She showed me a photo of the two of you. On your boat."

"Ah, yes, we both carry that one. So, did you like the *Willow?*"

"It's a great boat. I really enjoyed it."

"Good. Layla's a good sailor."

He grinned. "I noticed."

"I just wanted to stop and say—"

"Well, hello there!"

Bill's voice was full of that undertone Ethan knew so well; the testosterone was up. He couldn't blame him; one look at this woman would have most men on the rise.

"Bill Stanley, Stephanie Parker," Ethan said, yielding to the inevitable.

"Nice to meet you," the brunette said.

"Lovely to meet you," Bill cooed.

Stephanie smiled politely, but she turned back to Ethan. "I just wanted to say hello. Layla speaks very highly of you."

Ethan smiled, warmed by the simple words. "Thank you."

"Wait a minute," Bill said. "You're not...the friend she tried to set Ethan up with, are you?"

Stephanie's gaze flicked to Bill, then back to Ethan, her perfectly arched brows raised. "She tried with you, too?" Ethan nodded. "I told her no. Nothing personal," the woman added.

"Me, either. I said no, too."

Stephanie smiled, widely, and for a moment Ethan wondered if he'd been crazy when he'd made that decision. But at the time it had seemed far too rude to even consider it.

That was what he got, he thought now, for having been on the shoulder-to-cry-on end of his sisters' heartbreaks too many times; he'd been, they told him, almost decently sensitive to female feelings. From them, it was high praise.

"I told her she wasn't going to use me to escape," Stephanie said.

Ethan looked at her with interest. "Is that what she was trying to do?"

"I think so. She's shy with men when it's on a personal level. You...scare her, and there's not much that does."

"I really don't believe this," Bill put in, as if the sense of what they were saying had just sunk in. "You're turning *this* beautiful creature down for..." He lifted his hands and brows in an expression of utter disbelief.

Stephanie turned her gaze back on Bill. Uh-oh, Ethan thought. You stepped on it, buddy.

"For what, Mr. Stanley?" Stephanie asked.

"Well..." Bill said, sounding as if he might be vaguely aware he'd made a tactical error. "You two are... I mean, you're a goddess." He floundered, obviously thinking flattery was his way out. "And she's...well, she's a bit..."

"Layla has been my best friend from when we were both skinny little kids. She always will be." She looked Bill up and down as if he were something with too many legs to be in a clean restaurant. "And for your information, Mr. Stanley, I have no doubt that she could outlast you in a run, beat you at tennis, or ride your backside into the ground on a bike. And I would dearly love to watch."

Ethan bit his tongue; he would like to watch that himself. Stephanie turned to him, nodded. "Nice to meet you, Ethan."

Then she turned on her heel and, without a second look at Bill, walked away.

Ethan smothered a laugh; his friend looked stunned. Ethan sat, afraid his laughter was going to break loose. He found himself watching Stephanie as she left, found himself liking her for things that had nothing to do with her unarguably spectacular looks, things such as her loyalty, her sass and her refusal to overlook an insult to a friend, even from a stranger.

"Whoa," Bill muttered.

"Toasted you, didn't she?" Ethan chuckled.

"What the hell did I do?"

Ethan's chuckle died away. "She's Layla's friend."

"I know, but—"

"If you don't get it now, you never will," Ethan said.

And that, Ethan thought later, back in his office, was a definite possibility. Bill was smart, he was successful, he was a good-looking guy, but sometimes he was a bit slow on the uptake in his people relations. Always had been. Ethan had always thought of Bill's consistency, his unchangingness, as something to count on, something reliable in an ever-changing world. Now he wondered if it just meant Bill had permanent tunnel vision. Not to mention that it was a narrow tunnel. And for the first time he began to question their friendship.

He heard the phone ring, but with her usual efficiency Karen was on it by the second ring. He picked up his pen and went back to the spreadsheet printout the accounting department had dropped off this morning; he still liked to go through a hard copy so he could make notes with a pen. Not that he expected to find anything to question; they were too thorough. He almost wished he would find something, at least it might make him able to keep his mind focused.

I told her she wasn't going to use me to escape.... You scare her, and there's not much that does.

Stephanie's words echoed in his head, ruining his concentration once more. He scared Layla? He never scared anyone. He couldn't even scare his sisters, hadn't been able to even when he'd wanted to, when they were growing up and he'd been terrified something would happen to them if he didn't frighten them into being careful.

Just lunch? Oh. Okay.

The subtext was there, impossible to avoid. It was just

lunch, so it was safe. He wasn't in any danger of…what? Being misunderstood? By who? By Layla, or by anyone who might see them? Knowing Bill, he knew the answer to that one. Before he'd always laughed off Bill's remarks about never being seen with any woman less than an eight. It was just something a guy said, he didn't really mean it. Or at least he would set it aside if the right woman, who maybe wasn't that eight or better, came along.

With Bill, he wasn't so sure that would ever happen. And he was very much afraid that it was that way with a lot of men. Enough so that women like Layla hastened to back off, to set up men with their traditionally beautiful girlfriends….

She's shy with men when it's on a personal level.

No wonder.

But it was their loss, he thought. They would never hear that wonderful laugh, never laugh in turn at her quick wit, never feel their chest tighten at her gentle kindness, never stand in awe of her passion for her chosen cause, never wonder if that passion spilled over into other areas of her life….

He dropped his pen. He straightened. He stared out the office window at nothing.

He'd clamped down on that thought so swiftly it had startled him. He'd clamped down on it as if it were impossible, as if it were unthinkable.

As if he were as narrow-minded and unfeeling as Bill.

He sat there for a moment longer. Then he reached into his In box, fingers searching, until he found the pale blue envelope he was looking for. He looked at the address. Then he looked at the clock; it was nearly six. After a moment he got up, grabbed his jacket, tucked the envelope into a pocket and walked out of his office.

Marina del Mar was a small enough town that he found her house easily. They'd told him at her office that she'd left twenty minutes ago, so he knew she hadn't been home long. Her car, the sport utility he knew now that she used to bus people around when necessary, sat in the driveway of the small but tidy house, undoubtedly still warm. There didn't seem to be a garage, only a carport to one side. Then he realized it was a duplex, with another unit to the rear, perhaps that had been the garage at one time.

The little front cottage sat amid a profusion of furiously blooming plants, and even from here he could smell the sweet scent of flowers. He didn't know enough to know what kind he was smelling, but the fragrance was sweet, enticing and a lovely counterpoint to the fading warmth of a summer day. Others simply gloried in their own beauty, some low, fat, almost fluffy-looking, others, the ones he saw most of, long-stemmed and exotic-looking amid the profusion.

He parked behind her Blazer, then hesitated. He wasn't sure what he was trying to prove, or whom he was trying to prove it to, but he hated the idea that she might think he was holding back because he didn't want to be seen with her on a more formal basis. Even more, he hated the thought that it might truly be a factor.

He got out of the car and strode determinedly up to the door. Knocked. Waited. The door swung open.

She stood there, staring at him as if in shock.

He knew the feeling.

She looked...completely different. Gone was the austere suit. In its place, a pair of dark blue leggings and a blouse of some soft, shiny material that slid over her like liquid.

And her hair was down. It was longer than he'd ever imagined, almost to her waist, thick, wavy and lustrous. It looked like a fall of golden satin, and his fingers itched to touch it to see if it was as silken as it looked.

Nowhere to be seen was the severe, sometimes stern, totally controlled professional. In her place was the personification of the compassionate, gentle person he'd seen; she was softer, more vulnerable, less...armored.

And, in the glistening blouse, with one hand on her hip emphasizing a nipped-in waist, she looked not fat, not even big, but rather...voluptuous. Richly and lusciously curved. Womanly, he thought, a little startled at his reaction to the sight of her.

She tilted her head, looking up at him. She was barefoot, he realized; with her medium business heels she usually looked him almost levelly in the eye. Her hair slipped over her shoulders, trailing over the blouse like a streak of sunlight against a morning sky. He stopped his hand in the act of reaching out to touch an errant lock, but his fingers curled, wanting that touch.

He realized suddenly that he'd been standing there for...he wasn't sure how long, and neither one of them had said a word.

"I...got your address from your note," he said hastily, certain he sounded as rattled as he felt, but afraid he was going to say something as idiotic as "Gee, you look different...."

"I guessed."

She didn't sound any more at ease than he did, which, perversely, calmed him down.

"I hope you...don't mind," he began.

She seemed to come out of her own distraction and, in the way of someone just remembering her manners, said quickly, "Of course not. Will you come in?"

"I...thank you."

He stepped past her into what was apparently the living room. It was airy, inviting, full of bright colors set against white. It was as if all the color she denied herself in her business life exploded here in her home. He'd wondered if the dark, staid suits were her real choice or just a facade she hid behind. Now that he had what appeared to be an answer, he wasn't sure how he felt about it.

"Can I get you something? Soda, coffee?"

"Coffee would be nice," he said.

She nodded, gestured him toward the comfortable-looking pale yellow sofa and disappeared around a corner to where he presumed the kitchen must be. He sat, noticing the neat stack of magazines on the table, which was a striking piece of driftwood topped with thick, clear glass with what appeared to be a stained-glass rim. It was a unique piece, and he spent a moment looking at the table itself before he shifted to the surface. A couple of different gardening magazines, one on sailing, a consumer guide magazine, and, surprisingly, one that seemed dedicated to knitting. If she subscribed to any periodicals related to her work, she kept them out of the living room. Or perhaps she kept them at work, leaving her home as a refuge from the tragedy she fought daily.

He looked up as she came back into the room, two mugs of coffee in her hand. She set one down on the table in front of him. It was perfectly colored, with just a dollop of milk. And he was sure it would be sweetened just right, as well; she'd obviously paid attention when he had coffee at lunch.

"Is something wrong?"

Her voice cut through his distraction. "Uh, no."

She simply sat there, looking at him, waiting. In the moments it took before he found the words, he had time to wonder at himself, at how he, a usually calm and articulate guy, was suddenly having such difficulty speaking coherently.

"I just wanted to ask you…"

She had lifted her own cup to her lips, bent her head slightly to sip, and the golden curtain of her hair fell forward. It was the kind of hair that gave men hot, erotic dreams as they imagined it sliding over naked skin—preferably their own. It was the kind of hair that made fingers curl, as his did now. It was the kind of hair that went with the voice he'd first heard on the telephone, the voice that—

"Ask me what?"

He coughed to cover what was turning into chronic distraction and tried again. "I wanted to ask if…you'd like to go out to dinner tonight."

Her mug stopped in front of her mouth. That mouth. She

stared at him over the rim of the cup, as if what he'd asked was much more significant than it should have been. As if it meant everything he'd been afraid it would mean, that she knew, that she understood all the thoughts he'd been having ever since Bill had made him see what he was doing.

She wasn't answering. The silence stretched until he started to shift restlessly on the sofa. He should have prepared for this a little better, he thought, and rushed to say something. Anything.

"I thought we might go to the Sunset Grill," he said. "They have great food and a great location."

It was also one of the more romantic destinations in town. A restaurant with a light, airy feel and a design that made every table seem secluded and private. And Layla's expression told him she knew that perfectly well.

"Or someplace else, if you like," he finished, feeling as lame as he sounded.

Still she was silent. She set down her mug, and he didn't think he was mistaken; her hand trembled just slightly. When she lifted her gaze to his again, the only thing he could think of was a vivid memory of a teenage Sarah, terrified yet determined, standing at the edge of the high dive. Layla had that same look in her eyes. In those vivid green eyes that seemed to leap out at you when her hair was down in that incredible mass of gleaming color.

He opened his mouth to say something, anything, to ease her distress, when she suddenly answered him.

"I'd love to."

He found himself grinning. "Good."

She rose. "Let me change—"

"Why? You look fine." She looked at him intently for a moment, as if wondering if there was anything behind his words. Feeling as if something more were necessary, he added, "I like that shirt. It sort of shines."

He waited for her to laugh pityingly, as his sisters usually did if he ever dared to make some comment on their clothes.

Layla didn't laugh. Instead she murmured a barely audible "Thank you" and went to slip on some shoes.

He felt absurdly good. She deserved this. Not that dinner with him was any great prize, it wasn't that, but she deserved to be treated like any other woman he liked spending time with, not relegated to the middle of the day because of what others might think.

And besides, it had been a damn long time since he'd been out to a non-business dinner. It didn't have to mean anything other than that.

So why did he keep thinking it was going to end up meaning more? A lot more.

Ten

She liked this place, Layla decided. The food had been delicious, and the secluded booth, with its crisp white tablecloth and single red rose, was comfortable and had a lovely view of the harbor. They were close enough to speak without having to raise their voices, and she couldn't see another person in the place, nor could they see her, except in passing.

She liked it so much, she was even able to relax and carry on an almost normal conversation. At least, as normal as any woman could manage when sitting across a romantic dinner table from Ethan Winslow.

"How are your sisters?" she asked.

"Fine. Sarah's job hunting again, but that's pretty standard every time her boss gets on her nerves."

"I can't imagine working for a boss you hate," Layla said empathetically.

"Could be worse," he said with a crooked grin. "She used to work for me."

Layla chuckled. "Did she?"

"For a while. She said working for me was…stifling. I think that was the word."

"Oh, dear. I'm sure you didn't mean to be."

He lifted a shoulder in a half shrug. "It's just not her thing. She's more of an artistic type. She's happier now, for all her complaining." He seemed to hesitate, then added, "She liked you."

"Thank you. I liked her, too." She didn't say that one of the reasons she had liked Sarah was her unabashed adoration of her brother; she guessed he would just shrug that off, too. Sometimes men were very annoying.

"What about Margaret-don't-ever-call-me-Maggie?" she asked.

Ethan laughed at her use of the nickname. "Working way too hard and loving it. Although, she lost a little boy to leukemia last week, and she's taking it pretty hard."

"The good ones do, I imagine," Layla said softly.

"Yes. And she's definitely one of those."

He was genuinely proud of them, she thought, and she liked him all the more for it. "I can't imagine how hard it must have been for you back then, raising them like that, and you so young yourself."

He shrugged. "It had its moments." He gave her a sideways look. "I met your friend Stephanie today."

"So I heard." He lifted a brow at her, and she explained. "She left a message on my machine and said she'd run into you at lunch."

She'd also said several other things, most of which Layla wisely kept to herself. Especially the part where Stephanie had called Ethan's friend the King of Dorkdom.

But her endorsement of Ethan himself had been complete, and it was one of the reasons Layla had agreed to being here. She had a great deal of faith in Stephanie's judgment.

"She said you tried to play matchmaker with her, too."

Layla flushed. "I just thought…you two have a lot in common."

He looked at her as if he knew the exact reasons behind her efforts. Just as Stephanie had looked at her. Maybe they did both know, she thought ruefully.

But he merely asked, "Such as?"

You're both beautiful, she said to herself, knowing she couldn't speak it. "It was just a thought," she said, praying he would let it drop.

"Does she matchmake for you, too?"

"No. I don't date," she said before she thought. But he didn't point out that this evening very much resembled exactly that. Probably because that wasn't at all how he intended it, she told herself.

"Why?"

She shrugged. "I just don't."

"Ever?"

Why wouldn't he just let it go? "Not for a long time."

"Then you have."

She sighed. "I did, for a while," she said after a moment. "A couple of guys. And then, once, I was engaged. I met him when I was in college."

She heard the tightness that had entered her voice, but Ethan didn't. Or else he didn't care. "What happened?" he asked.

Better now than later, she supposed, and told him. "I tried to measure up—or rather, down—to what's expected of a woman in this society. I got there, and suddenly I had a full social calendar. Then I met Wayne Doucet. He was a sexy Cajun, and it was one of those…whirlwind things."

"Dangerous," he said.

"What was dangerous was what I was doing to maintain that image. Within six months of our engagement, I ended up in the hospital. My entire system was out of whack from my dieting. My doctor was furious, told me I was killing myself." She lifted her glass of iced tea as if it were champagne to be toasted, keeping her voice carefully free of any bitterness; she didn't really feel it anymore, anyway. "I finally had to accept that I would never be that female ideal."

He didn't seem to react, just asked calmly, "And when you did…?"

"I left the hospital, got fit and back to what my doctor said was a healthy weight for me, and…let's just say Wayne didn't let the door hit him on the backside on his way out."

Ethan said a single, two-syllable word, short, sharp and descriptive. Startled, Layla stared at him for a moment, then smiled.

"Close enough," she agreed. Then, feeling she'd bared her soul enough for one night, she asked him in turn, "What about you?"

He shrugged. "Once. I lived with her for a year or so, but it didn't work out. No time." Then, with a wry twist of his mouth, he added, "Which is what Sarah says is my problem. No woman's willing to play second fiddle to my work."

"Would she?"

"What?"

"Would a woman you really loved rank beneath your work? Or is always putting your work first just…a habit?"

He looked thoughtful for a moment. "I'm not sure. How about you?"

She blinked. "Me?"

"Everybody in your office says you work too hard."

"I work hard," she agreed, "but I don't know that too hard is possible when you really believe in something."

"And I," he said quietly, "would never argue with that."

And there, Layla thought as they finished and made their way to the parking lot, was the real problem with tonight. She *liked* him. She genuinely liked him. She almost wished—except for the sheer pleasure of looking at him—that he were ordinary-looking, just an average guy, instead of this striking, dark-haired, vividly blue-eyed example of masculine perfection. She wished he had a belly, or was going bald, or at the least had a crooked nose or something. Anything to take him out of that exalted plane and bring him down here with her.

But it wasn't going to happen. He was what he was, and he couldn't change any more than she could.

So why was she here? she wondered as they drove back to her house. Why had he asked her out tonight? Was it simply for company, a dinner out with somebody who understood nothing more complicated than that was involved? Did he expect her to understand, without it being said?

Even if she didn't understand, there was no misunderstanding that his work came first. He'd said that in so many words, after all. And any imaginings she had that that was only because he hadn't met the right woman, the woman to take his mind off constant work, were worse than foolish.

He walked her to her front door as if this were a real date.

More likely, she told herself as she fumbled with the key, he was used to looking out for his sisters and it was habit to make sure any woman got safely inside. He was, obviously, a gentleman. If he was anything less, they wouldn't be standing here, because he never would have made that ridiculous bid in the first place.

She got the door open and turned back to him to say thank-you and good-night. She caught him looking down at her—a novel enough experience for her—with an expression she couldn't quite put a name to.

"I…thank you. It was a lovely dinner," she said, rattled somehow by that look.

"You're welcome."

He kept looking at her. And she kept trying to figure out that expression. It wasn't puzzled, it wasn't surprised, it wasn't urgent, it wasn't contemplative, but it somehow was all those things, and something more. Something that made her think of carefully banked embers that were hotter than they appeared.

It made her edgy. She could barely take a breath. Desperately she searched for something—anything—to say.

"Sarah said I should take you sailing again," she blurted. "She thinks you need the break."

"I'd like that," he answered, his steady, unnerving gaze never wavering.

"I'll...see about the boat."

God, why was he staring at her that way? She had to do something, to move, back away, get away from those riveting blue eyes. Why wouldn't her muscles cooperate? Why were her legs frozen even as her knees felt wobbly? Why—

He bent his head and kissed her.

Layla nearly collapsed in shock, yet she knew this was what he'd been signaling since the moment they'd arrived on her doorstep. She just hadn't been able to believe it.

And then she knew nothing except the feel of his mouth on hers, gentle, warm, sweet....

A kiss on the forehead, or the cheek, she could have dealt with. Could have told herself it meant nothing but friendship, nothing but a more physical "I like you." Could have convinced herself it was meant to tell her just that, that it was liking, no more.

But this... This was so much more. At least to her, and the tiny voice screaming out a warning that she was a fool for thinking it meant what it felt like died in the ensuing heat.

She felt him start to pull back and almost wept with the loss. But then he made an odd sound and was back, deepening the kiss, taking her mouth with his in a way that made her dizzy.

At last, at the moment when she sagged against the door behind her, almost unable to stand, he broke the kiss. There was nothing baffling about his expression now. It was full of stunned shock.

I know just how you feel, she thought, but she couldn't form a coherent word. Could barely breathe.

He muttered something that sounded like "Later," although she knew there was more to it, and then he was gone.

Quickly, just this side of running, he was down the steps, up the walk and into his car and gone.

In some small part of her mind that was still functioning, Layla wondered how long it would take for her world to stop reeling.

It's quite obvious to us. He's losing his mind.
It's too bad, but there's nothing we can do.
How sad. He used to be so smart, so capable.
Now, now, don't be upset, you'll be taken care of.
The diagnosis is confirmed. He'll be helpless by the end of the year.

Ethan awoke with a start, sitting straight up in bed with a gasp. For a moment he stared into the morning gray of his room, afraid there would be some trace of the dream figures that had been hovering over him, taking his life away with their pitying words.

He'd almost gotten rid of the dream. He'd fought it hard, shoving it to the back of his mind, refusing to acknowledge it, denying he even remembered it on those mornings after the nights when it came to him.

But this time it had come back with a fierce vividness. This time it had wrenched him out of sleep and left him gasping for air. This time, when the condemned man in the dream had looked in the mirror, it had been Pete's face he saw. And then Ethan's own face. His mind had morphed the two images together until they could no longer be separated.

His subconscious, Ethan thought wearily, wasn't much on subtlety.

He fell back against his pillow, staring up at the ceiling he could barely see in the faint light of dawn. It was his own fault, he thought. He'd brought it on himself. If he hadn't resorted to thinking about Pete last night, this wouldn't have happened.

But nothing else had been strong enough to drive the other

thoughts out of his head. Thoughts about the utterly unexpected sweetness and fierce heat of kissing Layla Laraway.

He hadn't mean to do it. He'd fought the urge from the
moment he'd recognized it. But somehow, staring down at
her, at that soft mouth and those green eyes, he'd lost the
battle.

And he had a sneaking feeling he'd lost much more than
that.

Just the fact that thoughts of his mentor and what had
happened to him were the only thing powerful enough to
drive Layla out of his mind was enough to scare him—a lot.
He'd been startled enough that he was feeling attracted to
her; that the attraction had changed to arousal had shocked
him. That he had to plumb the worst and darkest part of
himself to combat the effects of a single kiss left him shaken
and confused.

He'd never felt like this before. Not just not this fast, but
ever. With Gwen he'd reached a pleasant comfortableness,
the ease of familiarity. He'd enjoyed sex with her, been content with that. He'd once, in college, had a more...heated
affair with a grad student who had, he learned later, taken
him on as her project for the year, but he'd never gone
through fire. Not like this.

And now he didn't know what to do. He hadn't been looking for this. Certainly never expected to find it, especially
with this woman.

But he had. There it was. And now he had to decide what
to do about it.

His gut instinct was to run. Which was unusual enough
that he sat there in the dawn and thought about it for a moment. Did he want to run because of the fierceness of it?
Because he knew Layla deserved more than he'd ever given
a woman before? Because he wasn't ready for this kind of
feeling?

You're thirty-five years old, Winslow. When the hell *are*
you going to be ready?

Even as he thought it, he knew it wasn't strictly fair. He'd spent the time in his life when most men would have been having a succession of relationships being a father figure to his sisters, working so hard at it that he hadn't had enough spare time to eat or sleep, let alone anything else. Even if there had been a woman who hadn't balked at the realization that two young girls were part of the package.

So it was only natural that he would still have to go through that stage, albeit a bit later in life than most. But still, it had been five years since Sarah had moved out on her own. Five years when he'd had to…make some changes in his life. He'd lived with Gwen, dated a couple of other women semi-seriously before that, and a couple not seriously at all since then. But never, with any of them, had he ever felt anything like this. And never would he have guessed it would come in such an unlikely package.

But it had. He couldn't deny that. No matter how good he'd gotten at denial lately.

And Pete's image plowed back into his mind. He closed his eyes, ridiculously, as if that could save him from seeing what the dream had forced him to look at.

What the hell had happened to his nice, quiet, ordered world? Sure, Sarah caused a ripple now and then, and there was the occasional business crisis, but for the most part his life had gone along smoothly, requiring from him only a bit of hard work, a lot of time and some mental exercise.

Then he'd answered his phone to hear the sexiest voice he'd ever imagined possible, and almost immediately his entire existence began to change.

She still had the sexiest voice. And it still sent shivers down his spine. And that hair, God, it felt so damn good to touch, and when it was down, spilling across her back, it was incredible. And those eyes, and her mouth…

He shuddered as the memory of how that mouth had felt beneath his rippled through him. Fighting the sensation, he glanced at the clock, decided he might as well get up and headed for the shower. A cold shower. Couldn't hurt.

"So, when are you going to see Layla again?"

Ethan grimaced at the telephone. He hadn't spoken to Layla since that night last week that was burned into his memory, but he'd been cornered by Sarah every day. Always with the same question.

"I don't know that I am."

"You haven't even called her yet?"

He smothered a sigh. "Phone lines go both ways, you know."

"Fine. I'll tell her to call you."

He went still. "You've been talking to her?"

"No, but I'm going to, if you don't get on the ball."

"Sarah—"

"You need a life, bro. All work and no play makes Ethan a pain in the butt."

"Yeah, yeah," he said; he'd heard this chorus from her before. Often.

"I thought you had fun sailing that day."

"I did."

"And all those lunches."

"Yes."

"I thought you liked her."

"I do."

"So what's the problem?"

I'm a coward? he suggested to himself.

"Ethan," Sarah began, then stopped. This was unexpected from his never-at-a-loss-for-words, never-hesitant sister, so he prompted her.

"What?"

"It's not...you wouldn't... She's not a small woman. You wouldn't let that...matter, would you?"

He thought of Layla as she'd looked when she'd answered the door. He thought of her on the *Willow*, her joy in the sail so clear on her face. He thought of her dealing with Mr. Kaplan so gently.

He thought of the taste of her mouth, the softness of her lips.

"I hope not," he said softly.

"I know you're not like that, that you don't think nothing matters but looks," Sarah said, sounding relieved. "I just hope Layla knows it. She's probably been hassled all her life. She might not believe anybody can see past it."

"I know," he said, even more softly. His little sister was smarter than he'd given her credit for.

"When I was in high school and put on that weight, you always told me I was still beautiful."

"You were."

"Layla's prettier and thinner than I was. And I'll bet she's smart, maybe even smarter than you."

Ethan's mouth quirked. "I won't argue that, since I'm not feeling particularly smart at the moment. So, is this going to be your new campaign?"

"Maybe."

Heaven help us all, he thought. When Sarah got her mind set on something, she was notoriously stubborn. She would push and prod and gnaw away at your resistance until you gave in simply to get her off your back.

He sighed as he hung up the phone. Maybe he should be glad. Maybe it would be easier if Sarah simply took things out of his hands.

But a few minutes later, after he'd broken down and called Layla to ask her to lunch so they could talk, he wondered if Sarah might not have more work cut out for her than she realized. Wondered if his sister hadn't considered the possibility that not everyone would agree her big brother was a prize.

Layla had turned him down.

Eleven

She'd done it. It was over. She should feel relieved.

So why did she feel as if she'd cut her own throat?

She'd expected to be upset, to be sorry, to be sad that the fantasy was over.

Instead she had been angry. At life, at fate, at the world that insisted on putting her on the outside. But most of all at herself; for again walking old, tired ground she'd long sworn off.

She had given herself three days. And then, with a stern "Snap out of it!" she had gone back to her life. Which had, she saw as soon as she walked into her office, gone on without her; there was a pile of mail and papers all over the desk she hadn't been around to defend.

She stood in the doorway, in the act of slipping her purse off her shoulder. She looked at the stacks on the desk. The stacks in her In basket. The messages piled by the phone.

She put the purse back on her shoulder. And walked right

back out again. She'd missed her last day at The Oaks; she would start there.

There, too, they seemed to have gotten along without her, although she was greeted warmly. Serves you right, she thought, for thinking you're indispensable. Maybe Stephanie's right when she says you should take more time off.

She made what she called her rounds, checking on their most recent referrals. She met with Mrs. Dorothy Tijera, the administrator, and caught up with things on that end. And then, against her better judgment, she asked the question she'd managed not to until now.

"I'd like to ask about another patient, Dorothy. Not one of our referrals, someone else."

"Oh?"

"Peter Collins."

She saw that Dorothy knew immediately whom she meant. "Oh, yes, very sad." She looked at Layla curiously. "What's your interest?"

"He's…a friend of a friend."

Dorothy frowned. "A friend of Mr. Collins? Odd. He's never had any visitors. I was under the impression there was no one."

"It's…a difficult situation," Layla said.

After a moment Dorothy nodded; if there was anything she'd grown used to in this place, it was difficult situations.

"Did you want to see him?" she asked Layla. "I've not been in his wing yet today, so I can do that now."

Layla hesitated. It was really none of her business. Especially now. But she was curious. She just wasn't sure about what.

"Just in passing," she finally said. "I'll walk along with you."

Dorothy nodded and rose to her feet. Layla followed her out into the hallway, wondering as they went if she was making a big mistake.

Of course, she was still wondering if she'd made a big

mistake in turning Ethan down, too. But it was just too risky a path to follow. She would do something stupid; she just knew it.

Dorothy used a key at her belt on the door that was kept locked to prevent wandering. It kept the patients in, but also caused the occasional problem when a patient became frustrated at being unable to open the door, their dying mind unable to grasp the concept of it being locked, or why.

"As I recall," Dorothy said, "Mr. Collins has been stable at late stage five for some time, although it's sometimes hard to judge at the later stages."

Her brows furrowed as she tried to recall. Dorothy had been running The Oaks since its inception, and she'd seen many patients over those years, but Layla knew she had amazing recall, so she simply waited.

Then Dorothy had it.

"He came in for testing with cognitive symptoms, when he couldn't balance his checkbook or understand the details of a contract he used to be able to commit to memory. When he started finding himself in strange places with no idea how he got there, he came in as an outpatient. Finally, when ADL became too much for him without assistance, he committed himself."

ADL, Layla knew, was shorthand for Activities of Daily Living, such as eating, bathing and dressing. "And now?" she asked.

"He still has short periods of lucidity, although less and less often. He can't remember where he used to live, or where he went to school, or sometimes even his nurse's name, when he sees her every day. Yet every once in a while he'll say or do something so…normal…."

Layla bit her lip. Her father had been a man much like Ethan had described his mentor. He had gone through the same process, the same slow deterioration. It had been agonizing to watch, and she truly couldn't blame anyone who wanted to avoid it.

Especially someone who'd been through what Ethan had been through, losing both parents, having to become one himself, managing to raise two young girls—and do it well— and push himself through college at the same time. He'd already accomplished more than many did in a lifetime.

A couple of minutes later she was standing in a doorway, looking at a still handsome but oddly dressed man—he had a bathrobe over twill pants and a plaid shirt, the robe itself not worn normally, but sideways, wrapped around his waist—who was talking animatedly to his own reflection in the mirror above the small sink in the corner.

This man had been a powerful, dynamic businessman, a man who had built W.C.T. from the ground up and made it into the successful business it was today. He'd been a groundbreaker in research and development in many different areas, a true renaissance businessman. And now...

Layla turned away from the door. Dorothy had not yet gone in, and she stepped back before the man saw her, her hand gently on Layla's arm.

"I know, honey," she said softly. "I know."

"Every time I think I'm used to it, something slams it home again. God, I hate this disease!"

"We all do. And someday, somehow, we're going to beat it."

Layla tried to concentrate as Dorothy gave her details on Pete's condition. When she got back to her office, she threw herself into her work, desperate for the distraction. She made herself concentrate solely on whatever was in front of her, pushing aside everything that wanted to hammer at her from outside that tiny spot directly in front of her.

It worked, some of the time. But every once in a while her guard would slip and she would think about her father. About Pete Collins.

And about Ethan.

He'd sounded...not startled, but merely puzzled when she'd so abruptly told him she was busy, too busy to see him, too busy to even talk about seeing him later. She knew, when she'd dodged telling him exactly what she was busy with, that he would guess it was just a ploy, that what she was really saying was that she wouldn't see him, period. He was too smart not to.

She wondered, as she gave up trying to scare up more work that simply wasn't there and left the office, if a woman had ever turned him down before. Surely no woman in her right mind would.

Which explained why she had, she supposed.

She pulled into her driveway, picked up her purse—she'd finished so much today that there hadn't even been anything to put in her briefcase and bring home—got out of the Blazer and walked up to the porch.

She almost tripped over the flowers before she saw them.

She stood there for a long moment, staring down at the vase full of soft greenery, the perfect backdrop to the array of beautiful, delicate, exotic lilies in various colors. Tucked among them was the florist shop card on the usual plastic trident.

Lilies. Her favorite flower. She grew them here by the porch and always tried to have a few in the house when they were in bloom. Which he had, it seemed, noticed.

She felt an incredible tightness in her chest. She'd turned him down, and he'd bought her flowers?

Whoa, girl, slow down. You haven't even looked yet. Maybe they're from somebody else.

As if there were anybody else who would even do this for no reason, no birthday, no holiday, nothing.

She should look. But she couldn't seem to move.

She opened her door. She stepped inside. Set down her purse. Hung her keys on the rack by the door. Turned. Stood there in the doorway, staring down at the vase of flowers.

At last, with an effort better suited to starting a long-distance bike ride, she reached down and picked them up. She carried them to the driftwood-and-glass coffee table and set them down. She took the small envelope from the holder. And stared at it almost as long as she had the flowers.

It was his writing; she knew it was. Her heart began to hammer in her chest at the mere thought of Ethan sending her flowers. Even after she'd turned him down. This was amazing, heady stuff, and she didn't have much experience with it.

Finally, she opened the card.

"You owe me another sail. You promised. Ethan."

Her mouth quirked wryly. Well. Wasn't that just as romantic as could be?

She laughed, suddenly and out loud, at her own silliness. Here she'd been afraid to even imagine they were from him, and now she found out they were, and instead of being happy, she was critiquing the message.

She was still chuckling at herself when the doorbell rang. The deliveryman, perhaps, needing a signature she hadn't been here to give? She threw open the door.

It wasn't the deliveryman, it was the sender.

"Ethan." It was all she could manage at the moment, although she was vaguely aware she should be saying something else. Thanking him. Something.

But she hadn't seen him for days, and she'd somehow convinced herself he wasn't as gorgeous as she remembered.

She was wrong.

He was dressed for the office, although his suit jacket and tie were gone, and the top two buttons of his pale blue shirt were undone. The sleeves were rolled midway up his forearms, accenting the strength and subtle power in his wrists, and the long-fingered elegance of his hands.

"May I come in?"

She gave a start. "I...of course."

She backed up, and he stepped inside. He wasn't cautious about it, he brushed her as he went past, although there was plenty of room for him to get by. She tried for some of the focus she'd exercised all day to steady herself, but it didn't seem she had much left. She did, barely, manage to speak.

"Thank you. For the flowers." She gestured toward the table where they sat. "They're beautiful."

He glanced that way. He nodded, then smiled rather ruefully. "I just pointed at the ones like you have outside."

"Lilies," she said. "Asiatic lilies, to be exact."

"That's what they said."

He walked over to the sofa and sat. Forcing her to do something similar or appear rude, she realized. But she let it happen. Face-to-face with him, all her resolve seemed to have vanished. The only safety she allowed herself was to take a seat in the single chair at a right angle to the sofa.

She waited, silently. She had to know what he had to say before she said a thing. After a long tense moment, he spoke.

"I'm not going to dance around this, Layla. I'd like to ask you something."

"All right," she said, relieved that her voice sounded much steadier than she felt. "Ask."

"Did I read you wrong, or when you turned me down Friday, did you mean...never again?"

Well, that was blunt enough. If he was going to be that honest, so would she. Well, almost. She could never, ever, tell him the real truth.

"Yes," she said.

He didn't look surprised. "What did I do?"

"Nothing," she said hastily, urgently. "It's nothing like that."

"Then why?"

"Ethan, I...you have to understand. It just wouldn't work."

"Why?"

Because, it would be too easy for me to fall in love with you.

Even as she thought it, she knew it would be the height

of absurdity for a woman like her to fall for a man like him. Rather desperately, she searched for the right words.

"You should be spending your time with somebody better suited to you."

"Suited?"

"Yes."

"I thought we got along rather well."

"Well...yes, we did."

"So what do you mean?"

"I just...you deserve a life for yourself, after raising your sisters."

"Okay. I agree. Your point?"

God, he was going at this as if it were a business meeting. Which only proved she was right, he didn't feel about her what he should feel about someone he was going to get...involved with. He couldn't.

"That you shouldn't be...wasting your time on something that can't...go anywhere."

He leaned forward suddenly, and she fought the urge to run. "Can't? You have a husband stashed away I don't know about?"

"No! Of course not."

"Then I fail to see the problem."

"Ethan, listen. We do get along. But you need somebody more...like you. Somebody like—"

"Your friend Stephanie?"

"Exactly. She's sweet, smart, vivacious, beautiful..."

Her voice trailed off as he leaned back against the sofa cushions, looking as if he'd just had a suspicion confirmed. "I see."

"I like you. I'd like to be...a friend. But—"

"Friends," he said with cool emphasis, "don't set each other on fire with one kiss."

Memories rushed back, memories of that night, of the heat, the fire, the startling explosiveness of it. Color flooded her face; she couldn't stop it.

"I see you remember," he said dryly.

As if she could forget, Layla thought. "I remember," she whispered.

"I knew it had to go both ways," Ethan said. "It was too fast, too hot, not to."

"Ethan, please—"

"What *is* it, Layla? What the hell made you run?"

"You ran first," she pointed out.

"Only because I hadn't expected it to be so hot so fast."

She flushed again; she could feel the warmth rising in her cheeks as the memory of the heat that had flashed between them rose in her body.

"Neither did I," she murmured almost to herself. In truth, she hadn't expected it at all.

"So, I wasn't wrong. It was the same for you."

She couldn't deny it. It would be a bigger lie than she could tell. "Yes."

"So why, Layla? Why the panic, the attempts to set me up with your friend?"

She sighed. She'd tried, she truly had. She'd tried to make it graceful, had tried to give them both an easy way out. But he wouldn't let it happen.

"Because," she said wearily, "I think we'd both get tired of being stared at while people try to figure out what a hunk like you is doing with a woman my size."

Ethan leaned back once more. He let out an audible breath. His mouth twisted slightly. "Sarah said that might be the problem."

Layla gaped at him. "You talked with Sarah about... this?"

"Not exactly. She just mentioned you'd probably have trouble believing it...doesn't matter."

Layla didn't know whether to be humiliated or furious, so she wound up a painful combination of both. She was afraid to open her mouth, afraid she would yell if she did. It took a long moment for her to steady herself.

"It does matter," she said, her jaw tight. "Reality is a thin-obsessed world, and if you don't believe that, then the turnip truck just left without you. If you don't understand, it's because you're beautiful and you've never been anything less than beautiful."

She appreciated that he didn't deny it. "And you don't think you are?" he said instead.

She gaped at him, knew she was gaping at him, but couldn't help herself.

"After our parents were killed," Ethan said quietly, "Sarah put on a lot of weight. Comfort food was her way of dealing with it. For a couple of years she was out of control. I saw what she went through. How…cruel people could be."

Her anger died unspoken. "She's…not heavy now."

"No." He looked at her steadily. "So, you think I'm a shallow, appearance-fixated idiot?"

"No!" Then, calmer, she added, "But I have a full-length mirror."

"I don't need a mirror. You *are* beautiful."

She stared at him. He'd sounded utterly sincere.

"And I don't mean all the usual stuff, that you're smart, and kind and compassionate, and that that makes you beautiful. Although it's all true. I mean beautiful in the literal sense."

Layla was having trouble breathing. Uttering a single word was beyond her. She could only continue to stare at him. It wasn't that she hadn't been told all this before. She had, in fact. But never like this, or by a man like Ethan.

She watched as Ethan's expression became one of bemusement, his eyes growing unfocused, as if he were looking inward.

"I mean it," he said, sounding a bit surprised himself. "I just realized I've been looking at women I would have found attractive once, and all I can think of is how skinny they are. Downright bony. Painfully bony."

"Ethan," she whispered, barely able to hear it herself.

He focused on her suddenly. He looked at her for a long silent moment. She felt a bit dizzy, then realized she was holding her breath. She let it out, slowly, only vaguely aware that she was shaking her head; whether in negation or awe, she wasn't sure.

"Come to dinner with me," he said suddenly. "No more casual, safe lunches. Dinner. Dress up. I'll even put my damn tie back on."

No, her common sense ordered.

Yes, her heart shouted.

It was going to hurt even more when the inevitable happened. He might think now it wouldn't matter, but let him see the stares, let his friends start teasing him—as she guessed the friend Stephanie had met already had—let him see, eventually, a photo of them together, and he would realize the absurdity of it.

But in the meantime...

In the meantime, for just a little while, she could live the fairy tale. She'd never wanted or expected a knight in shining armor, and she wasn't sure what tale Ethan might have ridden out of, but for a while, she could live it.

The temptation was too much to resist.

"I'll go change," she said softly. She got to her feet and for a moment basked in Ethan's pleased smile.

Move over, Cinderella.

Twelve

"He what?"

"I kid you not," Ethan said, grinning as he tugged the cover over the mainsail and snapped it. "He's suing them."

"He uses a toaster to thaw out his frozen money, then sues the toaster company when he forgets it and it catches fire?"

"Yep."

Layla sighed. "Sad to think that there's a village somewhere missing its idiot."

Laughter burst from him. He'd laughed more in the past week than he could remember doing in years. He loved her sense of humor; it was just the tiniest bit askew, and made him laugh both at the quips and the delivery. The entire day had been a joy, more relaxing than anything he'd done since the last time they'd gone sailing. Now they were pleasantly weary, finishing the cleanup on the *Willow*.

"Just tell me he didn't win the lawsuit," Layla said, sliding the main hatch closed and locking it.

"It's still pending," he said. "So I didn't tell you any of that."

"Any of what?" she said with a grin.

Yes, Ethan thought, she did make him laugh.

Over the past week he'd found himself calling her for the least reason, sometimes to ask her opinion on something, sometimes to tell her something he'd heard, and sometimes just to hear her voice.

Odd, he thought; her voice was no less sexy than it had ever been, but he heard it differently now. There was no trace left in his mind of the sultry, petite brunette he'd conjured up when she'd first called him. Her voice was pure Layla, and when he heard it, he thought of her laugh, her smile, and the way those green eyes of hers sparkled with laughter or warmed with compassion.

He'd enjoyed every minute spent talking to her this week. He'd had a wonderful time in her company today. He'd decided she was the most fun he'd had for a very, very long time.

What he hadn't done was kiss her again.

He told himself it was because he didn't want her to back off again. That what had sparked to life between them in that single kiss had scared her. But he had a sneaking feeling he'd been just as scared. Just as shocked.

He'd almost convinced himself it was a fluke, born out of a long time without and a need to show her he appreciated all those things about her that made him feel warm when he thought about her. Maybe she had thought it was a fluke, too. Maybe she had chalked it up to…something else.

But they were going to have to find out. Soon. He was spending altogether too much time thinking about doing it again, about finding out if the flaring heat had been an…accident, or if they were dealing with a genuine fire hazard.

He thought about it as they finished up on the boat. As

they gathered their gear and headed up the gangway to the parking lot. As they loaded the things into his car.

Layla grew uncustomarily quiet once they were in the car. He'd sensed all day that there was something else beneath the smile, the laugh. They were away from the marina and halfway back to her house when she hit him with it.

"I need to tell you something."

His stomach tightened instinctively. They'd been doing well all week, she seemed to be learning to trust him. But her tone was that of someone afraid that what she was about to say wouldn't go over well.

But she would say it, if she felt she should. If he'd learned nothing else about her, it was that she didn't shrink from difficult tasks that needed to be done.

"What?" he finally managed.

"I...saw Pete."

Startled, he glanced at her. "You what?"

"I was making my visit to The Oaks. I had a meeting with Dorothy Tijera, the administrator, a couple of weeks ago. So...I asked about him."

A couple of weeks ago. After she'd backed away from him. When she hadn't meant to see him again. But she'd still asked about Pete.

He glanced at her. "Why?"

She looked slightly uncomfortable. "I...thought you might want a first-hand report on how he was. And I could do that for you."

So I don't have to. So I don't have to face reality.

She didn't say it, and there wasn't a trace of disapproval or judgment in her voice.

No one had ever tried to stand between him and reality before. He didn't quite know how to feel. Pleased? Comforted? Honored?

All of those, he thought. What he didn't feel was anger, anger that she'd done it, and that surprised him a little. Even he knew he was touchy about the subject, and he didn't quite understand why what he would have considered a trespass by anyone else wasn't bothering him. Perhaps he was just too astonished that she had done it, given the timing.

"Maybe I shouldn't have—"

"No," he said, interrupting her. "No, it's all right." Then, after a moment, and a steadying breath, "How is he?"

"Physically, he's still doing fairly well. He can still feed himself, simple foods, but he's not sleeping well. I'm afraid that's not unusual in stage five to six dementia."

He made himself ask. "And…the rest?"

He felt her looking at him, and after a moment she said, "Are you sure you want to hear?"

"I'm sure I don't," he said grimly.

"Then don't feel you have to, just because I…butted in. I just thought you might want to know that, physically, he's still in fairly decent shape."

"Considering," he muttered.

"Yes."

She didn't deny the finality of it, didn't sugarcoat it for him. She was, in this as in everything, honest. But she was also thoughtful and considerate and wouldn't force him to hear anything he didn't want to. Which, perversely, made him want to.

He pulled into her driveway, behind her Blazer. Parked. Turned off the motor. And finally turned in his seat to look at her.

"Go ahead."

She hesitated, then said, "Some typical signs. He's become obsessive about brushing his teeth. Does it repeatedly throughout the day and often gets up at night to do it. He's taken to talking to his reflection in the mirror."

Ethan winced. And reminded himself that he'd asked.

"I know it hurts, Ethan," she said softly.

"I know you know."

It was the only reason he could stand what she'd told him at all. She'd been through this, to the bitter end. She knew.

But she, unlike him himself, had stuck it out with her father. She, unlike the proverbial rat on the sinking ship, hadn't abandoned him to his fate. Guilt, the enemy he'd battled for three years now, flooded him.

He couldn't speak, couldn't get a word out past the tightness in his throat, his chest. He yanked the door open and began to unload her things from his car in sharp, jerky motions. Layla said nothing, merely got out and began to help, grabbing her tote bag and the sack with cheese, crackers and a sandwich and a half left over from their day on the water.

She quickly put the food away, then headed back to get the tote just as he was coming in with it and closing the front door. It clicked shut, and he leaned against it. Suddenly he felt more than just pleasantly tired, he felt exhausted.

"He told me to stay away," he whispered.

"Did he?"

Ethan nodded, slowly. "The first time he found out I'd been there and he hadn't known me. He told me not to come back."

Layla crossed the three feet between them. He could smell her scent, something light and sweet, a subtle counterpoint to the tang of saltwater and wind. She'd pulled back her hair as usual today, but a few tendrils had escaped, and this time she hadn't efficiently smoothed them back into place.

"I should have gone, anyway. I shouldn't have listened to him. But I...wanted to. Wanted an excuse not to face what was happening to him. Not to face that I was going to...lose him, just like I'd lost my parents."

"I know," she said softly.

And then she was hugging him, her arms enfolding him as if she wanted to shelter him from reality physically as well as mentally. And the words "pleased," "comforted" and "honored" suddenly didn't say nearly enough.

He wrapped his arms around her and held on. He felt a shiver go through him and didn't know if it was a reaction to what she'd told him or a response to her closeness.

But, whichever it was, he felt…soothed. And the tightness in his chest eased. For a long time he simply stood there, leaning against the closed door, his eyes shut, soaking in her warmth.

She felt…good. Sunshine warm. Soft, yet not. Solid, but he could feel the taut muscle under his hands. Just…womanly. Lusciously curved. Her figure, he realized, was nicely proportioned, it was simply on a bit larger scale. And it was out of her control, just as being six foot one had been out of his.

He opened his eyes. Tilted his head so that his cheek rested atop her head. Her hair was soft against his skin. He let out a long, quiet breath, feeling himself relax as he did it.

After a long time he lifted his head. Layla looked up at him, and he saw a world of understanding, remembered pain and compassion in her eyes.

Time spun out between them, silent, invisible, yet as real as the wind that had propelled the *Willow* today. And then his gaze shifted to her mouth, to the lips that parted slightly even as he looked.

Now, he thought. Find out now.

He lowered his head. She didn't pull away, and he felt an odd certainty that she, as much as he, wanted to know if it had been real or some one-time collision of need and deprivation.

It had been real.

Heat kicked through him, along nerves that had nearly atrophied, along nerves he hadn't even realized he had. Her mouth was soft, hot and welcoming. She tasted sweet and erotic at the same time, and his body leaped at the combination.

He traced her lips with his tongue, and she opened them for him. He probed, suddenly voracious, needing, wanting, demanding more. She gave it without question.

His hands slid up from her waist, pressing her close. He could feel the soft swell of her breasts, full and lush against him. He thought he could feel the tight nubs of her nipples but couldn't be sure, because need cramped him so furiously he could only groan against her mouth.

He had to be sure. He slipped a hand between them, pulling back to allow himself access. Slowly, carefully, giving her every chance to pull away or stop him. She did neither. And then he was cupping that voluptuous, yielding flesh, lifting it, savoring how it rounded into his hand. He groaned again, unable to stop himself.

His thumb slid up and over the rigid peak. She cried out, a hot, swirling sound of pleasure that made his entire body tighten. His hips moved convulsively, arching into her, his own rigid flesh trapped wonderfully between them.

Layla moaned, rubbing against him. Her hands moved to his chest. For a moment he thought she meant to push him away, but instead she simply touched, smoothed her fingers over him, caressing, and he wished his shirt was gone, so that he could feel the contact with his bare skin.

Already he was hovering on the edge of his control, and in some part of his rapidly fogging brain he was aware that nothing like this had ever happened to him, so hot, so hard, so fast.

And then Layla went from welcoming to demanding, tasting him back, stroking his lips, probing past the ridge of his teeth, then dancing over his tongue with hers. Fire ripped through him, taking his breath away. But he didn't care, he didn't need to breathe, anyway, not as long as he had her in his arms.

Only when the room began to spin around him did he step back. He stared at her, at green eyes that seemed alight from within with that heat that had seared him, at those perfect lips now swollen from his mouth. He became vaguely aware that he was breathing rapidly, that his heart was hammering, that the pounding in his ears was his own racing pulse.

Layla Laraway had set him ablaze with a single kiss. And

judging by the dazed, wondering look on her face, the flames had singed them both.

He guessed he had his answer.

"Sure, you can borrow the bike," Bill said. "I don't need it for a while."

Ethan wisely kept silent on that as they loaded the expensive mountain bike into the trunk of his car; he'd known Bill long enough to realize he had to have things, whether he used them or not. Whatever was the current fad, Bill had to have the biggest and best, be it bicycles or ski equipment or stereo systems.

"So, is it a race, or what?"

Bill was also competitive and frequently turned even the most casual of activities into a contest.

"No. Just a ride."

"Oh, yeah?" Bill leaned against the fender. "With who?"

"With a friend," Ethan said, dodging.

Bill brightened. "A girl? Did you get smart and change your mind about the little brunette?"

"No."

"Then who—" He broke off, and gaped at Ethan. "Not the—not your auction date?"

His jaw set. "Yes."

"You're still seeing her?"

"Yes." He eyed Bill warningly. "In fact, we're going to dinner tonight."

Bill shook his head in bewilderment. "I don't get it."

"No, I know you don't."

"Why? I'm the one who has to fight for the good-looking women. You could have anybody, so why…?"

Bill had the sense not to say what he was thinking, but Ethan still didn't answer. Didn't think it deserved an answer. Bill was thankfully silent as they fastened the trunk lid over the bike. As Ethan rechecked the bungee cords, Bill crossed his arms over his chest—as if expecting a battle—and looked at Ethan.

"Boy, she must be something special in bed."

Ethan jerked upright, staring at his friend. For a moment he couldn't speak, in part out of shock, and in part out of the sensation that had rippled through him at the idea of finding out just what Layla could do in bed.

"You know," Bill explained, "like an ugly woman who learns how to really please a man because that's her best shot?"

Ethan's mood shifted instantly at the cruel words. Images of Layla flashed through his mind, of her at the wheel of the *Willow,* of her gently breaking the news of Pete's condition to him, of her staring up at him after one of those kisses that nearly fried his circuits.

"What I know, ol' buddy," he said through clenched teeth, "is that you need a serious attitude adjustment. And I'd better get out of here before I make that adjustment with my fist."

He left Bill gaping after him, looking like a landed fish. Although right now he seemed to Ethan more like a snake. And he wondered again why he put up with him, if the years made up for this blind spot he'd never noticed before. Wondered if he was clinging to the friendship because it was a last remnant of the life he'd lost.

Shoving his friend's shortcomings out of his mind, he headed home. Layla was going to meet him there in the morning, and they were going to take the bikes up into the foothills for a ride. He was a beginner at off-road biking, so she'd promised to take it easy on him and take him to one of her favorite yet easier trails.

She must be something special in bed.

He'd tried not to think about it. He knew she was still tentative about him; he sensed her holding back, keeping some part of herself still hidden and protected. Even in the midst of those explosive, almost lethal kisses they now reg-

ularly indulged in. Kisses that were about to drive him out
of his mind.

They'd overheated themselves every time; they'd caressed,
stroked and downright groped each other furiously, and yet
still they held back. It wasn't just her doing; it was his, too.
He knew his own reasons—he told himself she needed time,
needed to learn to trust him, that he didn't want her to regret
anything—but he wasn't sure if her reasons were the same.
He only knew that the hesitation on her part was always
there, and so he managed, barely, to call a halt before he
completely lost control.

But he didn't know how much longer he could manage it.

They'd been to dinner three times, dinner and a movie
twice, they were taking the bike ride tomorrow, and he was
working up to asking her to come next week when the family
gathered for Margaret's daughter's birthday. He thought she
would say yes. There was still that annoying split second of
hesitation whenever he asked her, as if she had to think about
every time they saw each other, but in the end she said yes,
and that was what mattered.

But what mattered most was knowing he'd been right; her
size wasn't important to him, at least not anymore. But she
had been partly right, too. Yes, he'd noticed the sideways
looks they got, noticed the puzzled expressions on some
faces, but he didn't care.

As for Bill... For Ethan, today had been the final straw;
his relationship with his old buddy would never be the same
again.

Sarah, on the other hand, was delighted. And couldn't wait
to tell Margaret their brother was finally getting a life.

He felt as though he did have a life, for the first time in a
very long time. And it was Layla's doing. She made him
laugh, she made him relax, she made him look forward to
each day for more than just whatever challenge work might
bring.

And she was quite possibly going to drive him mad in the
process.

* * *

Layla stared at herself in the mirror. She dropped the towel she'd wrapped around herself after her shower. And stared again. Nothing had changed, no miracle had occurred. Her curves were still there, rounding her into something far removed from the bodies plastered all over every kind of media. The fact that many of those bodies looked anorexically unhealthy didn't change the reality.

Bony. Painfully bony.

Ethan's words made her smile, and she dressed hurriedly. He was due in twenty minutes, and it took that long to dry the mass of her hair, let alone put on a bit of makeup.

Her hair was still damp when he arrived, but it would finish drying quickly enough out in the warm summer morning air. They were taking her Blazer so they could load both bikes inside, so he'd parked out on the street to keep her driveway clear. By the time he got to the door, she had herself fairly well together.

At least, she thought she did.

Then Ethan swept through the door without a word, pulled her into an enthusiastic embrace and kissed her breathless. But then, all his kisses left her breathless.

And scared her senseless.

She'd never known it was possible to feel this way, she thought later as she drove along the familiar route to the hills.

Admittedly, her experience was limited, but she'd always thought her relationship with Wayne had been satisfactory enough while it had lasted. Now she knew better. Now she knew about flying. About instant fire. About wanting so badly nothing else mattered.

And they hadn't even made love.

Yet.

She knew it was up to her. Ethan had never pushed her further than she wanted to go, and she knew he would never take it to the next step without some signal from her that she was ready.

Was she ready?

More important, what if she held back so long that he got tired of waiting? It was amazing enough that he seemed to want her. Rather intensely. How could she risk it? How could she bear it if he turned away now?

If she'd been smart, she would have stuck to her guns and stayed away from him. But she'd been unable to resist the chance to live the fantasy, even if only for a while.

Because she knew, eventually, it would be over. Ethan was kind, generous, sensitive, all those things. But sooner or later some woman would come along, some woman who suited him, and it would be over. Oh, he would do it gently, and he would probably genuinely feel bad, but nevertheless, there she would be.

So there was only one thing she had to decide, she thought as they reached the narrow, winding road, thankful that she had a reason not to chatter now. She had to decide which would hurt more, having painful memories of sweet intimacy lost, or having no memories at all to treasure.

She suddenly remembered something Stephanie had told her once, when contemplating a new man in her life, something about what she called the equation. "I take the time we would be together and divide it by how long it will take me to get over him when he's gone. If it comes out less than one, I'm gone."

She had a feeling that in her case, the numbers would be all on the wrong side of the decimal point.

She also knew it didn't matter. She'd already decided.

Thirteen

"Stephanie wasn't kidding."

Layla looked at him curiously as he followed her into the kitchen and collapsed onto one of the oak chairs at her table.

"What?"

"That day I met her. She told…my friend you could ride his backside into the ground on a bike. I believe her."

She laughed. They had done more than she'd planned today, but Ethan had seemed to enjoy it. He was the one who had pushed for more, until she knew they weren't going to make it home before dark. And they hadn't. But she refrained from reminding him of that.

"A bit tired?" was all she said as she began to gather things for the spaghetti dinner she'd promised him.

"I'm whupped," he drawled.

"Then you could have picked a more comfortable chair to sprawl on. Or the sofa."

"I'm too sweaty. I need a shower before I sit on anything else."

"Feel free. Plenty of towels on the shelf in the bathroom."

"Wanna join me?"

Layla froze. He'd said it lightly, teasingly. She shouldn't take it seriously, she told herself. But he'd said it. He'd never done that before. He'd never even joked about them becoming…more intimate.

"Sorry," Ethan muttered, and she heard him get up. Heard footsteps as he headed for the hallway to the guest bathroom.

"Ethan?" She heard him stop, made herself turn to face him. He was looking back over his shoulder at her. "Was it a joke?"

For a long moment he just looked at her. Then, finally, he said, "It was whatever you want it to be."

And then he was gone.

Layla set down the pot she'd been about to fill. For a moment she simply stood there. She looked down at her hands, resting on the edge of the pot, and noticed they were trembling.

It was whatever you want it to be….

She heard water start in the bathroom. He'd never showered here before. And she hadn't appreciated the fact enough, hadn't realized the images that would haunt her when he did, images of him naked and wet and gleaming….

She shuddered. She let go of the pot. *Now or never… Now or never… Now or never…* ran through her head like some desperate mantra.

She almost ran down the hall to her bedroom. She slipped out of her own worse-for-wear clothes and dashed into her own shower; silly as it was, she couldn't bear to do this with the disadvantage of starting out sweaty herself. She was in and out quickly. She toweled off, grabbed her robe and hastily pulled it on. She stepped back into her bedroom.

And couldn't make herself go on. Besides, now the water had stopped from the other bathroom. She'd had some idea, inspired by shower scenes in books and movies, of romantically slipping in to join him, as he'd said. Some stupid idea…

She sank down onto the edge of her bed. Right. As if she would have the nerve to bare herself like that, in the cruel, too-bright fluorescent light. She felt ridiculous even now, sitting there in the relative safety of her own room, in her green satin robe.

"Layla?"

She heard him, but couldn't answer. Couldn't move.

When she heard his footsteps coming down the hall, she stilled, one hand clutching her robe closed at the neck, the other clutching one of the uprights of her four-poster.

"Layla? You okay?"

He sounded worried. She sat there in the growing darkness, feeling like an utter fool. Moisture pooled behind her lids. She blinked it away furiously, angry at herself for so many things she couldn't even enumerate them at the moment.

And then he was in her doorway, wrapped only in a towel. She'd forgotten to ask if he had any clean clothes. If not, she would need to wash what he'd worn today so he could put them back on. He *had* to put them back on, or she was going to go stark, raving insane. Just looking at him, silhouetted by the hall light behind him, was close to making her crazy.

"Why are you sitting here in the dark?" he asked.

"I—I'll be out in a minute," she said as evenly as she could, silently telling herself that if she sniffed audibly she would slit her own throat.

It didn't seem to matter that she managed it. He came in, anyway, sat beside her. His closeness, the muscular expanse of his near-naked body, made her dizzy. "What's wrong?"

"Nothing."

For a moment he didn't speak. Then, "You've never lied to me before."

She sighed. "I know. I'm too lousy at it."

He slipped an arm around her. "Yes," he agreed, and she couldn't help grimacing. "What is it?"

"Oh, nothing. Just some silly idea of taking you up on your…invitation."

"My invi—" He stopped suddenly. He went very still. "You were…going to join me?"

"I should have known better. Should have known I couldn't pull it off. I'm no good at things like that."

Ethan took a deep breath. And again he didn't speak for a moment. She couldn't blame him; what was there to say? Whatever he did say was going to hurt her feelings, no doubt. Most anything would, she was feeling so raw right now.

"Then," he said at last, "what you need is practice."

It was her turn to go still. "Practice?"

"Lots and lots of practice," he said softly.

He reached out, tucked a finger under her chin and turned her face toward him. In the fading light of the room she could barely see his features, but she could feel his gaze on her as surely as if it were a physical thing.

"Layla?"

She couldn't miss the meaning in that single whisper of her name. Couldn't miss the portent in that gentle touch.

Slowly, so very slowly, she reached up and laid her palm against his cheek. His own hand shifted until he was doing the same.

"I was afraid you were kidding," she whispered.

"I wasn't. I wouldn't. I just wanted you to…have an out. If you wanted it."

"I don't."

"You're sure?"

"I'm sure," she said with a little nod, knowing he could feel the motion even if he couldn't see her clearly. "And…prepared," she added, then wished she hadn't as color flooded her face and she knew he had to feel the heat of it.

"Prepared as in…protection?"

She nodded again. Ethan chuckled. It was a wry, rueful sound. "Lady, I've been prepared for a week. I didn't have much faith left in my self-control."

Layla shivered at the heartfelt confession. And shivered again when he pulled her into his arms, holding her tight against him, as if he were savoring the feel of her.

She felt his hands on her, stroking, sliding over the slick satin of her robe.

"Oh, boy," he murmured. "You're...naked under there, aren't you?" Her breath caught, but it was enough answer for him apparently, because he groaned. "I haven't been six-teen for a long time, but, woman, you make me come to attention as fast as if I were."

Layla shivered again; the thought of being wanted like that was heady stuff. When it was this man, it was almost un-bearable.

Ethan rolled behind her and pulled her down beside him on her bed. She succumbed to the urge she'd buried for so long and lifted her hands to his chest. Her skin nearly sizzled at his heat, and her fingers tingled at the feel of sleek, smooth skin, roughened just slightly with a sprinkling of hair.

He felt as beautiful as he looked.

Her hands moved as if of their own volition, stroking, searching. Her fingertips found the flat nubs of his nipples, and instinctively she circled them, rubbing over the puckered flesh. They tightened at her touch, and she heard him make a low, hungry sound.

She stopped, somehow frightened.

"Don't stop," he said huskily.

"You like that? Being touched there?" she asked shyly.

"I like you touching me," he corrected. "Anywhere."

She blushed, grateful for the shadows to hide in. Thankful he hadn't insisted on turning on a light, she touched him again. And again. And he made that low, thrilling sound again.

Her hands slid down his sides, until she hit the edge of the towel knotted at his waist. She stopped.

"Anywhere," he repeated in a harsh whisper. And then, when she didn't move for a moment, he reached down, undid the towel and let it fall away. Heat surged through Layla, making someplace low and deep inside her cramp with need. When he put his hand over hers and slid it down his hip, that inner clenching came again, and this time she moaned under its force.

She wanted to touch him. Wanted it more than she could remember wanting anything in years.

"Ethan," she breathed.

"Touch me," he said; it sounded like a plea.

He wouldn't force her, but that tone in his voice made it impossible not to do as he asked. Her hand slid lower, then around.

She nearly gasped as she found him, hot, hard and heavy against her palm. And smooth. So incredibly, impossibly smooth. He did gasp, deep in his throat, as her fingers closed around him.

"Yesss!" he hissed.

Tentatively she stroked him. Then, as his hips moved convulsively, again. And again.

Somewhere amid her fevered haze she was aware that he was naked and she was not. Aware that it was probably intentional, that he was baring himself first, for her sake. He'd never made a move toward the tie of her robe, never even suggested she remove it. He was taking all the risks here. For her. Knowing she would be hesitant to take them herself.

Suddenly she felt like a coward. And hated the feeling. Especially when she had the safety of darkness to hide in.

And the pleasure of touching him so intimately, of tracing that rigid flesh, knowing that it would soon be inside her, part of him made part of her, aroused her beyond worrying about it anymore.

She yanked the knot of her robe free and wriggled furiously out of it.

Ethan panted out her name and pulled her against him. He groaned as if the feel of her naked skin against his own was the greatest pleasure he'd ever known.

Layla couldn't think any more about her misgivings, her qualms. She couldn't think anymore at all. She could only feel. Could only feel Ethan's body against hers, and now his hands on her, stroking, caressing, probing. It seemed furiously fast, but her body responded just as quickly. Responded to his hands cupping her breasts, then lifting them for his mouth, to his lips kissing that rounded flesh, to his tongue flicking that achingly tight peak until she nearly bucked in fierce response. To his other hand sliding down her body, slowly, teasingly, parting the silky curls below her belly, probing, to the first touch of his fingers on her already need-slickened flesh. To the first slow, tantalizing caress of that knot of nerve endings that made her cry out in shocked wonder.

She, who had spent most of her life thinking her mind was all she had to offer, became a mindless, driven thing, at the mercy of the hands and mouth and body of a man she would never, ever have thought to have.

He lifted himself over her, whispered her name as he handled protection with hands that were trembling enough to give her a deeply feminine thrill. It was all she could do to wait for him to finish before she reached for him, pulling him to her.

He probed for a moment, too eager to go slow. She didn't want him to go slow, she wanted this so badly she could barely breathe, and if he didn't do it now, she was very afraid she was going to scream.

And then he did it, sliding into her with an ease that betrayed her readiness and a swiftness that made her body lunge upward in response. But she screamed anyway, helplessly, mad with it now, certain she could bear no more. Then he began to move, electrifying her with his fervency and with the low, guttural sounds that broke from him at the depth of each driving stroke.

She grabbed at him, clutching the taut curve of his buttocks. He pulled back, almost leaving her as he looked down into her face. Sweat sheened his skin, his eyes gleamed even in the shadows, and intensity fairly radiated from him.

"Did I...hurt?" he asked, as if those were all the words he could manage.

"No!" she exclaimed instantly, aching with the loss of him. "More. Harder."

A low, muttered oath escaped him. He slid his arms under her, curled his strong hands back over her shoulders. The instant Layla realized he was bracing her, her body clenched fiercely. And then he drove forward, hard and deep, and she cried out his name. He pulled back, then drove into her again, and again, with a force that exhilarated her.

She could hear sounds that should have embarrassed her, sounds of flesh against flesh. They didn't; it was Ethan's body slamming into hers. She heard cries that also should have embarrassed her, breaking from her own throat in a voice she barely recognized as her own. They didn't; Ethan's groans of pleasure echoed her own.

And then she heard him say her name once more, in an awed, pleading, urgent voice that pushed her toward the final peak. She rocked her hips, forcing him deep, rocked again, savoring the sweet pressure of man and woman joined.

The sudden swell of sensation, rippling, surging, made every muscle in her body tighten. Including those clasping the welcome invader. She heard Ethan cry out as she clenched around him. He stroked her with his body once more, and she was flying, riding the billowing sensation that swept through her. She heard him groan again, this time as if it had welled up and burst from him in the same way his seed poured into her body. His hands tightened bruisingly on her shoulders, but she didn't care. His hips hammered into her one last time, and she reveled in it as the wave broke over her and she could hear nothing but his cry of her name, feel nothing but heat and pleasure and Ethan's arms around her.

Ethan roused slowly, lazily, completely unlike his usual swift awakening. He dug his head farther into the pillow, feeling cozily warm and comfy and not at all inclined to even look to see what time it was. It was still dark, that was all that—

Layla.

No wonder he was feeling like wet spaghetti. She had blown every circuit, flamed every nerve, in his body.

He turned his head. She was beside him, warm, close. Her breathing was soft, barely audible.

She was awake.

He could see that her eyes were open. But then she closed them. He lifted his head slightly. She didn't move.

"Layla?"

She sighed, then opened her eyes again. God, no, she wasn't regretting it, was she? Regretting the wildness with which they'd first come together? The tenderness that had followed the second time, when he'd been determined to make it last and last? He had, too. She'd been fairly writhing before he'd finally given in to his own body's demands and ended it.

Just thinking about it made him want her again, but he had to first find out why she was awake. Even if he didn't want to know.

"Are you…all right?"

She turned to look at him. "I'm fine."

"But you're awake."

"I'm not used to…sleeping with someone."

"Me, either. We'll learn."

He thought he heard her breath catch and wondered why. He reached over and toyed with a strand of her hair. He'd known that last night she'd been afraid, afraid he would find her unattractive. Instead he'd found her soft and warm and inviting, gloriously rich and luxurious.

He wished he had the words to explain, to tell her. But right now, he couldn't think of a single one.

So he kissed her instead. Long, deep and hot.

Layla kissed him back, the same way.

This time, afterward, she slept.

Fourteen

The tap on her back kitchen door startled Layla out of her contemplations. For an instant she thought it might be Ethan—and just the thought sent a frisson of heat down her spine—that he'd forgotten something when he'd reluctantly left to take the bike back to his friend. But she discarded the thought; he never used the back door.

Then it suddenly struck her that it was Sunday morning— barely, since it was after eleven—and time for brunch with Stephanie. Although they were always in touch, they had a standing date the first Sunday of every month for a long, uninterrupted talk. And since Stephanie lived only two blocks behind Layla's house, she often walked and came in from the alley, using the pathway beside the rear unit.

Layla went to open the door.

"Hey, girlfriend! What's up?"

"Hi," Layla said.

She hadn't even thought about what she would say to her friend. She'd been wallowing in the luxury of feeling pretty, feeling sensuously female, feeling wanted by the most beautiful man she'd ever seen.

And memories of just how beautiful he was made her, for the moment, mute.

"Where do you want to go for brunch?" Stephanie asked as she walked in, apparently not noticing Layla's lack of conversation. All too quickly she spotted the book open on the kitchen table, walked over, looked at it, frowned, then turned troubled eyes on Layla. "What's this for?"

Layla sighed. She'd dragged out the old book just moments before Stephanie had arrived. "I was just...looking."

Stephanie's frown deepened. "At a diet book? Why?"

"It's an old book," Layla said, trying to dodge the question. She should have known better; Stephanie didn't distract easily.

"I thought you swore you'd never try that again, never risk your health for something that's impossible."

"I did, but—"

"You said after you got out of the hospital that any man would just have to take you as you are."

Layla couldn't help it, she blushed furiously at Stephanie's choice of words as she recalled all the ways Ethan had taken her last night. He'd been immensely patient with her hesitation, hadn't quibbled with her need for darkness to hide in, and he'd made her feel, for those exquisite hours, completely beautiful.

She knew she was in trouble when Stephanie's brows went from furrowed to arched in a split second. The brunette studied Layla's face, then glanced down slightly at the open neck of her shirt. And Layla remembered suddenly the reddened mark Ethan's morning stubble had left on her skin.

"Well," Stephanie said. "Well, well, well. Did I just miss Ethan?"

"Barely," Layla said, seeing no point in denying what her friend had clearly already guessed.

Stephanie grinned delightedly. "Yahoo! Good for you, girl. It's about time."

Layla wouldn't have thought her blush could get any deeper, but it did. She could feel it, heat spreading anew up through her cheeks.

"You are being careful, aren't you? Condoms?"

God, would this blush never stop? Layla wondered. "Yes," she managed to say.

"So…how was it?" Stephanie asked, her grin widening.

Apparently not, Layla thought as even more heat rushed to her face.

"That good, huh?" Stephanie teased.

Layla swallowed tightly. "Better."

"Woo-woo!"

Layla couldn't help but smile and roll her eyes at her friend's joyous enthusiasm.

But her smile faded as Stephanie reached down and slapped the diet book closed. She picked it up and waggled it at Layla rather fiercely. "And I'd like to point out that Ethan apparently likes you just the way you are."

"He likes me," Layla admitted, "but…what if he's just…putting up with the rest because of it?"

"This is the Ethan Winslow of W.C.T., right? CEO extraordinaire, leader of industry, that Ethan Winslow?"

Layla looked at her suspiciously. "So?"

"I find it hard to believe that *that* Ethan Winslow would 'put up' with anything if he didn't damn well want to."

Stephanie's voice was stern, but it was the oath that really got Layla's attention; Stephanie never swore.

"Don't sabotage yourself, Layla. You thought you'd never find a man who would care for *you,* not what you looked like. And now here he is. It's time," she said, even more sternly than before, "to put up or shut up."

Stephanie's words echoed in Layla's head all during their brunch. She couldn't deny that there was a certain amount of truth in them.

But deep in her heart, she also doubted Stephanie could really understand how she felt.

"When are you seeing him again?" Stephanie asked as they left the small coffee shop they frequented on these occasions.

"This afternoon. It's his niece's birthday."

"You're meeting the family?"

She nodded, biting her lip; she was horribly nervous about it. "They'll all be there."

"Good sign, good sign!"

"Easy for you to say," Layla muttered; she doubted Stephanie had ever been apprehensive about meeting anyone in her life.

"It'll be fine. You like kids, they love you, you'll be with Ethan, so no problem. Have a good time."

Layla sighed.

As it turned out, she did have a good time. While Ethan gathered what seemed like a huge pile of gifts, Sarah took charge of Layla, dragging her through the chaos of ten children under the watchful eye of Margaret's husband, playing a game that seemed to involve spoons and cotton balls, to the kitchen to meet Margaret. The harried mother of the birthday girl was in an apron, and her nose was smudged with flour. She looked nothing like the dedicated physician Ethan had described, and Layla couldn't help smiling. Margaret's eyes reminded her of Ethan's, although they were a bit more gray than his vivid blue, and her hair was raven-dark, just like his.

"So, you're Ethan's Layla? He's spoken of you often."

Ethan's Layla. The words made her shiver.

"He's told me about you, too," she said, recovering. "He's very proud of you."

"I'd be nothing if not for Ethan," Margaret said bluntly. "He made it all possible."

"And will he let you thank him for it?"

Margaret eyed Layla carefully. And then, after a moment,

she smiled widely. "No. Welcome, Layla. I'm glad you came."

They talked for a while, there in the kitchen. Margaret was curious about her work, and Layla was glad to talk of something that didn't make her nervous. Without much thought, she pitched in as they chatted, helping set up plates for cake and ice cream, fastening rubber bands on party hats bearing the likeness of a certain ubiquitous purple dinosaur.

Squeals of childish delight came from the other room, punctuated by some odd electronic noises. "That'll be Ethan's doing," Sarah said. "He no doubt brought Megan the latest of her personalized computer games."

Margaret laughed and said to Layla, "He has one of his techie people write them. She's so spoiled. She's the only little girl who stars in her own adventure games."

Layla was charmed. It must have shown, because Sarah grabbed her arm and pulled her out into the family room, where the kids were gathered. And where Ethan, she saw immediately, had his niece on his lap in front of the computer in the corner. They were intent on an animated game that seemed to involve a herd of adorably chubby ponies and a little girl who did look a lot like Megan.

Layla felt her throat tighten as she watched.

"He'll make a great father," Sarah whispered to Layla. "If he ever gets in gear and gets around to it."

Yes, Layla thought, he will. It was obvious.

"He needs to give up being *our* father first," Margaret said. Then, with a sideways glance at Layla, she added, "Maybe you can help him with that."

Layla wasn't sure what to think. Here she was barely able to absorb the idea of being with Ethan at all, and his sisters were talking about kids?

Apparently, Ethan was having no such problem; once the video game had been turned over to the partygoers, he made no effort to act circumspectly in front of his family, often sliding up behind her for a hug or to plant a kiss on her ear.

He seemed to like doing that, and the slow, stroking movement as he pulled her hair out of the way seemed as much a part of it as the kiss itself. She couldn't help being embarrassed, but the family didn't seem to see anything amiss.

Stephanie called her the next morning to see how it had gone. Her friend was delighted with the idea of the personalized computer game and agreed it was a wonderfully sweet thing for an uncle to do.

She did not, however, understand Layla's misgivings.

"You liked the sisters, right?"

"Yes."

"And they liked you?"

"They seemed to."

"And the kid?"

"She's sweet."

"So what's the problem?"

"I don't know," Layla said honestly.

"What you need to do is lighten up, girl. Listen to Mother Stephanie now, will you? You need to remember how to just have fun."

"I do have fun."

"Good. It's been a long time coming for you. Enjoy, honey, enjoy."

Enjoy.

Layla thought about that recommendation a lot over the next weeks. Ethan took her everywhere she'd ever wanted to go, and a few places she'd never even thought about but enjoyed, anyway. He'd shown her the family albums, which were, he admitted, a bit skimpy, since film and the time to take photos had been a luxury. The sight of that struggling young family, Ethan trying to look older than his years, brought moisture to her eyes.

He bought her things, not grandiose, expensive things designed to impress a woman, but little things that showed a lot of thought, things specifically for her, books she'd wanted to read, exotic flowers, and one day he had the fuel pump on her car repaired without her even knowing it. He made her feel valued by asking her opinion on many things and more than once taking her carefully considered advice.

And in bed, he made her feel beautiful, adored and incredibly sexy.

So what was her problem?

She didn't know. She only knew she couldn't completely let go of her fears, her suspicions that this was all some sort of fantasy, that one day she would wake up and it would be over. Or, more likely, that Ethan would wake up, look at her and ask himself what on earth he'd been thinking.

It never seemed more like a fantasy than on the night of her thirty-first birthday. He took her back to the Sunset Grill, to the same booth their first dinner had been in. He ordered champagne, and strawberries dipped in rich chocolate for dessert. And then he took her on a moonlight cruise of the bay in a small rented, powered gondola, complete with singing gondolier—with, amazingly enough, a good voice.

When they went back to her house, he magically produced three wrapped packages. The first and smallest was an envelope containing tickets to a photography exhibit she'd mentioned wanting to see. The second was a small golden sailboat pendant, simple, and not expensive enough to make her feel uncomfortable.

The third, largest box contained a gift that startled her. It was a hooded cape, calf-length, in a rich, fine wool that draped beautifully. It was also a brilliant blue, a brighter color than she ever wore.

She didn't quite know what to say or do; it was so unlike her own conservative taste that his choice of it made her uneasy. But when he urged her to go to the full-length mirror in her bedroom with it, she couldn't think of a reason not to. So she did, and let him drape the cape around her.

"I knew it would look like that," he said softly as he lifted her hair free and let it fall forward over her shoulders.

She was afraid to look. But finally she had to. And she stared, stunned into total silence.

It was a dramatic garment. Very. And she had the feeling it would dwarf anyone lacking her height. But it was the color that startled her the most; it made her hair gleam like molten gold, and, to her surprise, turned her eyes a deep aqua that seemed to leap out at her from her own reflection.

"I—it's…amazing."

And it was. It was striking. It was head-turning.

And never in a million years would she have the courage to pull off wearing it. She'd spent her life trying to fade into the background. Wearing something that shouted confidence and high self-esteem, that demanded "Look at me!" was beyond her.

She thanked him, but she could tell he sensed it wasn't wholehearted.

Later, when he slid into bed beside her, he pulled her into his arms and said, "It's all right, Layla. You'll wear it someday. When you know you can. I just wanted you to have it for when that day comes."

How had he come to know her so well? she wondered.

And then he kissed her, and she knew the time for thinking and knowing had passed. She still thrilled at the feel of his long, naked body beside hers, shivered at the feel of his hot, sleek skin, and was nearly mindless with delight at the freedom he gave her to explore, to touch. Whatever she wanted, he told her, offering himself up to her, urging her hands and her mouth on whenever she would hesitate with uncertainty.

And he would touch her in turn, heating her blood so quickly and so fiercely that most of the time she forgot to worry about her body's imperfections. It was hard to think about such things when Ethan gave every evidence of being hungry for her all the time.

It was still so hard for her to believe.

But in the hot, dark hours Ethan made her believe it. Made her believe it when he undressed her with such care she felt

almost fragile, a feeling utterly foreign to her. And he made
her believe it when he began to stroke her in that slow, mad-
dening way that drove her crazy with a need she had never
known, never dared to acknowledge.

Had never dared to risk.

He whispered to her, soft, sweet words she had never
thought she'd hear. Words about beauty and silk and softness, words about curves that fit him so well.

And he made her believe.

He lay facing her, cupping her face in his hands and rain-
ing hot, sweet little kisses from her brow to her jaw and back.
And then her doubts didn't matter. She slid her hands over
his skin, knowing with joy in her heart that her touch was
welcome.

No, was craved, she amended silently as he arched himself
toward her as if he'd been waiting all day for her hands on
him. She took the gift he offered her, stroking him, tracing
the incredible male size of him with fingers still learning, still
inquiring. And no matter what she did, where or how she
touched, he let her know he liked it, sometimes urging her
to use more pressure, or a gentle squeeze.

And all the while he was returning the favor, his hands
stroking over her as someone stroked the finest silk, with
care, with a feather touch, and with mutterings of awe. That
anyone would feel that way about her amazed her and sent
her pulse racing nearly as much as did the gentle, coaxing
caresses.

When his mouth went to her breast, when he took one
nipple between his lips and flicked it with his tongue, rational
thought fled. A wave of hot, liquid sensation rippled through
her, and, paradoxically, she shivered under its force.

"Layla," Ethan murmured, then suckled her other breast.
She shivered again, and she thought she could feel him smile
against her skin. Then he spoke, and she could hear that smile
in his voice. "I love the way you respond to that."

As if she had any choice, Layla thought, when the heat of his mouth set her on fire. She couldn't think of a thing to say, she had no easy vocabulary, no practiced lines, for this. But Ethan seemed to understand her incoherent moans and continued on his path, finding sensitive spots with his hands and mouth, making her quiver under his honeyed onslaught.

She wondered, for an instant, if her fiery reaction was because of how long she had done without any sensual touching in her life. But then Ethan whispered in her ear, his deep, husky voice sending a new shiver through her, making her shoulders tighten.

And then his hand slid downward, parting the curls between her thighs. She knew the moment he touched her that she was already slick with her need for him, and when his probing finger found and stroked that knot of nerves, she had no mind left for words, and no breath left to speak them.

But Ethan didn't seem to mind; he growled something she wasn't even sure was a word and stroked her faster, gently increasing the pressure until she was crying out his name.

She reached for him, pulled at him, and he read her signal, sensed her urgency. He slid his hand down her leg to her knee and pulled her leg gently over his hip, opening her to his slow, sweet invasion. She savored the gradual stretching of her body as it adjusted itself to this welcome intruder. She savored the gentle rocking motion he began, each arc driving him deeper, stretching her wider. She savored the grip of his hands, holding her for his strokes.

But most of all she savored the way his breathing became audible, the way his heart hammered beneath the fingers she pressed to his chest, the low, guttural groans of pleasure he made with every thrust. That it was she making him feel like this gave her a pleasure that catapulted her over the edge so quickly she would have been embarrassed had it not been so glorious.

But it was. It was totally utterly glorious, and when he

gave an arching shudder and cried out her name, she thought she just might believe forever.

But that was before the light of day.

It was like this every time that he spent the night in her bed. She slept surrounded by his warmth, happy, content, utterly satiated from a night of all kinds of passion, hot and fast, or slow, smooth and lingering.

And then she would gradually awaken. Become aware of his arm around her, his hand resting on the belly that should be flatter, or the hip that was too wide. And the tension would begin to build in her again.

She would wiggle away from him, sitting up, clutching the sheet to cover herself in the sunlight. He would stir sleepily. She would stare down at him, at his powerful male beauty, and wonder what on earth he was doing here with her. Wonder what she had done to end up with this gorgeous man, burnished gold and dark against her crisp, pale yellow sheets, in her bed and in her life.

And wondering yet again when the fairy tale would end. Not how, that was a given, but when.

And every morning she scrambled out of bed to dress before he could see her naked in the unforgiving light.

"Take me in with you."

Layla stared at Ethan, clearly wondering if she'd heard correctly. Since they were standing in front of The Oaks, the place he'd sworn never to set foot in again, he couldn't blame her.

"Yes, I mean it," Ethan said, answering her unspoken question.

"Now, after all this time, you want to go in? You want to see Pete?"

No, I don't want to at all. But I have to. It's time. It's past time.

"Yes," he said determinedly.

He'd been thinking about it a lot lately. Hell, he'd been

thinking about it ever since Layla had made him feel slightly smaller than a flea about it. He'd become almost certain that this was the barrier he sensed between them, that this was what kept Layla from letting down that last wall. She knew he was still a coward about this, so it was no wonder she hid part of herself from him.

He'd stalled again and again. But now, time was up. He couldn't put it off any longer. If she could deal with it, with facing the memories of her father's lingering death, and do it every day, he could surely face it at least once himself. So he'd gone to her office, found she was already on her way over here, and sped across town to catch her in the parking lot.

He couldn't shake the feeling that he had to do this, not just for Pete, but for himself, for himself and Layla. It was as if he didn't deserve her, and how much she'd brought to his life, unless he at least matched her courage in this.

"You don't have to do this."

"Yes, I do," he said. And, gritting his teeth, he turned and led the way to the front doors.

Once inside the lobby, he was ready to run again. He was barely aware of the greeting from Dorothy Tijera. He was barely aware of anything except the hammering of his heart and an odd hum in his ears as they walked down a long hallway.

Although he did notice it was more like an apartment hallway than a hospital hallway; the floor was carpeted instead of linoleumed, the walls a cool, calming green instead of hospital gray or beige. Plants sat on side tables here and there, and pieces of what looked like original art of all kinds and all levels of competence were hung along the way. He vaguely remembered Layla saying something about trying to make the place as homelike as possible, that it seemed to help the patients. And that they let the residents decorate, giving them a feeling of at least some kind of control in their lives, which also seemed to help.

But right now nothing was helping him. When they

stopped in front of a doorway, he had to fight to suppress the urge to run. The last time he'd come here, before Pete had been moved into this long-term-care wing, he'd sworn he would obey his mentor's request and never come back. He'd felt as alone that day as he had the day the police had come to their door to get the three children who hadn't yet known they were orphans.

But he wasn't alone now. As if she'd sensed his thoughts, Layla slipped her arm around his, taking his hand, grasping it firmly, supportively.

He wasn't alone. Layla was here. He could do this.

Dorothy opened the door.

The man sitting in the chair by the window was barely recognizable as the dapper, together businessman he'd once known. His hair was all gray now, and mussed, where it had always been neatly combed. He had on a shirt and sweater, but over pajama bottoms. And dress shoes, with white socks.

Misery welled up in Ethan, and he bit his tongue against a cry of rage at this travesty, this destruction of a once vitally alive human being.

They went into the room. Layla had offered to wait outside, with Dorothy, but he'd asked her to come with him. To at least be in the room.

The man in the chair looked up. The eyes that had once been the epitome of laser efficiency were vague, confused. But still, they brightened when he saw them.

"Hello."

Ethan couldn't find his tongue.

"Hello, Mr. Collins," Layla said.

The man looked at her. "Do I know you?"

"No," she said, "but I hope you don't mind a visit, anyway."

"No, no," he said heartily. "Come in. My wife was just here, you know."

Ethan winced; Pete's wife had died a decade ago.

"I brought a friend with me," Layla said, gesturing toward

Ethan. Reluctantly, Ethan stepped forward, so Pete could see him.

The man frowned, stared. Then, unexpectedly, he said, "You look like the Winslow boy."

Ethan's breath caught. "I…am the Winslow boy."

"No, you can't be, he's just a youngster. Barely twenty. But he's a sharp one. He's going to go a long way."

Ethan didn't know what to think, how to feel. It was such a strange combination of being remembered and not remembered, he didn't know what to say.

"Don't try to convince him," Layla whispered in his ear. And then, turning back to Pete, she said gently, "Is he?"

"Oh, yes. I can pick 'em. I knew first time I saw him he'd be the one. In a few years he'll be my right-hand man. He's got it all, brains, drive, spirit. Better yet, he kept his heart. He's been through hell, but kept his heart. He'll be the one to run things after I'm gone, you'll see."

"I'm sure he will," Layla said.

Ethan knelt in front of the man's chair. Pete's gaze shifted back to him. The now-silver brows furrowed. "You surely do look like him."

"Thank you," Ethan said, not knowing what else to say. He felt Layla's hand on his shoulder, soothing, comforting. "Do you know what…the Winslow boy would like to tell you, Pete?"

"No, what?"

"He'd like to tell you how grateful he is to you. How much he owes you for giving him a chance, the chance that let him keep his family together. How he's thankful every day for what you taught him, not just about work, but about life, and what's important in it."

The smile that spread across Pete's face made it suddenly unimportant whether he recognized Ethan at all. Layla had been right; he'd been going at this all wrong. This wasn't for him, it was for this weary old man, who was losing his final battle. And if it hurt him to see his old mentor this way, so be it. As long as he could bring this smile to his face, he would be here. No matter what it took out of him. It was the least he could do.

It wasn't until they were outside, in the fresh, warm summer air, that he really looked at Layla. Her eyes were suspiciously moist as she looked up at him.

He'd done it, he thought. He'd actually done it. The last stumbling block between them was gone. Surely the way she was looking at him meant that.

"That was…a good thing to do," she said softly.

"I had to. Not just for him, not even just for me. You watched your father die of this…stinking thing, and you face it every day. I felt like such a coward, in the face of that kind of nerve."

"We all deal with things differently. We each have to—" She stopped, staring at him, as if his words had just now registered. "Me? You did this…because of me?"

"I never would have, if you hadn't come along. He would have died alone, and I would have carried the guilt for the rest of my life."

She seemed unable to speak for a moment, but finally asked, "And now?"

"I'll see him. As often as I can. Whether he knows me doesn't matter. You were right, Layla. It has to be for him, not me."

"You're an amazing man, Ethan Winslow," she whispered. "I'm proud to know you."

He looked at her intently. This wasn't the place he'd planned to do it, but the timing seemed right. And maybe the place was right; this was what had started them down this path, after all.

He took her hand and pulled her to the small bench situated amid a profusion of flowers at the side of the walkway. He sat and tugged her down beside him.

"I…" he began, but had to stop when his throat tightened unbearably.

''What, Ethan?''

She was looking up at him, traces of tears still welling in her eyes.

He swallowed and tried again. ''Proud? Do you mean that?''

''I do,'' she said, her voice soft and ringing with sincerity.

''Then…marry me.''

For a moment she just looked at him. And then she paled, as if he'd slapped her.

''Marry you? You…you can't mean that.''

''What?''

''You can't want to marry me!''

Ethan was having trouble keeping up. He'd thought everything was fine now, that she'd only needed him to face what he hadn't had the nerve to face. And now it seemed as if there was something else entirely that was wrong, something else that was responsible for the withdrawal he sometimes felt in her.

''Why not?'' he finally asked, hoping for some answer that would make sense of his confusion.

''I won't change, Ethan. I can't.''

Ethan went rigidly still. A chill crept over him. He'd thought this dragon had been slain long ago. ''What are you saying?''

''I will be this way forever.''

She said it almost warningly, and the chill that had enveloped him changed form, became an icy kind of anger he'd rarely felt in his life.

''So what have you been doing all this time? Waiting for me to change my mind? To wake up, to walk out, to decide I don't want you because you're not one of those anemic-looking females the media continually rams down our throats?''

She didn't answer, but he saw the flicker in her eyes.

''My God,'' he said tightly, ''you have been.'' He jumped to his feet.

"Ethan," Layla said, the tears that had threatened before flowing now.

"I can't believe you. I've done everything I can to convince you that what I want from you is between your ears, not measured on a scale. I don't know what else to do."

Layla lowered her head. Her hair, which he'd finally convinced her to wear loose now and then, fell forward in a golden, shimmering mass. Ethan remembered how it had felt sliding over his body the night she'd given him the most intimate of kisses for the first time. He shuddered, but his anger was ascendant, and he brushed off the sensation.

"I love you. *You.* As you are. It's you I want, not some phony ideal of a woman who's got no substance at all. When you can believe that, come find me."

He turned on his heel and walked away, leaving her there and not daring to look back.

Fifteen

Layla ignored the knocking on the door. There wasn't a person in the world she wanted to see, except one, and she knew he wasn't going to show up. Until now, they hadn't gone eight hours without at least talking on the phone. Now it was more than twenty-four hours since he'd walked away. Twenty-four long hours without a word.

Soon it would be dark again. And again she wouldn't sleep, again she would weep.

She tried to tell herself it was for the best, that it would have happened, anyway, eventually. But Ethan's words rang in her head like a death knell.

I love you. You. *As you are.*

Tears welled up and over again, as they had so many times during the long, lonely night. And she couldn't quite shake the feeling that she'd destroyed her blissful paradise with her own silly hands.

The knocking came again, and this time she heard a voice calling through the closed door.

Stephanie.

Lord, the last thing she needed right now. But she knew Stephanie would not give up and go away. So, reluctantly, she rose and unlocked the door. Without speaking, she turned before the door swung open and went back to the chair she'd been huddled in.

"Are you all right?" Stephanie demanded, shoving the door closed behind her and storming into the living room. "Are you sick? Your office said you hadn't shown up, hadn't called."

"I'm not sick." At least, not that way, she added silently.

"Then why—" Stephanie's words broke off abruptly as she came around the chair and saw Layla's face. "My God, what's wrong? You never cry like this."

"Welcome to Layla's world of firsts," she said, unable to keep the tinge of bitterness from her voice.

Stephanie was silent for a moment, considering. Layla could almost feel her friend's mind working swiftly, and thought rather inanely that any man who underestimated the lovely brunette's brainpower was a fool.

"Ethan," she pronounced after a moment. "It has to be Ethan. What happened?"

Layla sighed. "I love you, you're my best friend, but it's between me and him." She winced inwardly as she consciously did not use the word "us."

"Right. Now tell me." When Layla didn't respond, she plopped herself down onto the arm of the sofa and leaned toward Layla's chair, hovering like a predatory bird. "You're going to in the end, you know that, so let's cut the persuading and save some time."

It was true. No one could resist Stephanie when she was intent on something. And she knew her friend had only her best interests at heart. Layla made another halfhearted attempt to fend her off, then surrendered. She told her what had happened, fighting back the tears she was so unused to crying. Fortunately, Stephanie didn't interrupt her, in fact said nothing except "Go on" a couple of times when she faltered.

When she'd finished, Stephanie was still for a moment. Then she stood, walked across the living room, turned and came back. Finally she planted herself in front of Layla.

"I never thought I'd say this to you, but you're an idiot."

Layla's head came up sharply. Stephanie was glaring at her in a way she'd never seen from the woman who had been her friend since childhood.

"Has Ethan ever told you you needed to lose weight?"

"No, he—"

"Has he ever treated you less than wonderfully?"

"No, but—"

"Has he ever made you feel unattractive?"

Layla blushed. "No."

"He told you he loves you. As you are."

"Yes, but—"

"Yes, but? So what are you saying? You think he's a liar?"

"No!"

Stephanie knelt in front of her, her voice softer now, not so strident. "Layla, listen to me. Nobody knows better than I what you went through to get to where you are. I was there, remember?"

"I know." It came out brokenly; Layla knew the tears were about to burst free again. "You've always been there for me."

"And I'm here for you now. I always will be, just like you will be for me. But it breaks my heart that you finally learned to accept yourself, but you don't trust anyone else to do the same."

"I...just can't see how he could..."

"Because he's drop-dead gorgeous? Come on, girl. You've told me his history. That's a guy who has his priorities straight."

Layla couldn't deny that, so she said nothing. Stephanie was also silent for a moment.

Then, very softly, and seemingly irrelevantly, she said, "Do you know what 'Ethan' means?"

"What?"

"The name. Do you know what it means?"

"No. You're the one who pays attention to that stuff."

"Yes, and I looked it up. It's from the Latin and means 'constant.' Maybe you should think about that. Think about it hard. Because it sounds to me like you're the one with the problem about looks. Not him." Stephanie straightened. "I'll call your office and tell them you're not sick."

"Thanks," Layla said, glad to be relieved of that problem. She didn't know what else to say.

But Stephanie did. And she said it just before she walked out the door.

"If you blow this, you're a fool."

And then she was gone, leaving Layla sitting in a morass that had only gotten thicker and deeper. Was she the one with the problem? Was she, in her own way, as judgmental as others had always been about her? She recoiled from the idea, but she couldn't deny it outright, and that frightened her.

She didn't move, just sat there as it grew later and later. She made no move to turn on a light, was barely aware of the growing darkness. Her mind was no longer racing, it was spinning out of control, wildly caroming from point to point like a berserk billiard ball. Each point seemed to be something Ethan had said, and the remembered words sent her thoughts careering in another direction.

He'd gone to The Oaks. For her, as much as anything. *I felt like such a coward, in the face of that kind of nerve,* he'd said. As if he'd felt he had to do this to…what? Be worthy of her? Now there was an absurd idea.

I don't need a mirror. You are beautiful. An even more absurd idea.

What I want from you is between your ears, not measured on a scale. She could believe that. She'd always thought it, after all, that her mind and her dedication and her energy were all she had to offer. She'd just never thought it would be enough, not for a man like Ethan. And now she couldn't believe it, because if she did, she would have to admit the enormity of what she'd thrown away.

So you think I'm a shallow, appearance-fixated idiot? She knew it wasn't true, but that was still a huge step from…loving someone who didn't fit the norm.

I've been looking at women I would have found attractive once, and all I can think of is how skinny they are. Downright bony. Could it be true? Could a man really think that way?

I love you. You. As you are. He'd said it, in so many words. Declared it. And she'd thrown it back in his face, refusing to believe—

I never lie, and I keep my word, Ms. Laraway.

Even his sister had said it, that he'd taught them to be honest.

Honest. Meaning what you say. Not lying.

The spinning, the careering, stopped. Because she finally realized that the bottom line was very, very simple.

Ethan Winslow was not a liar. Not about anything.

He loved her.

Layla went very still in her chair.

For a long time she simply sat there, absorbing the revelation. The joy of believing warred with the fear that she'd ruined it all with her stubborn refusal to accept.

She was terrified that she might be right, that Ethan had finally given up for good.

But she couldn't live with not knowing. Couldn't not try, not when there was the slightest chance.

It was late, nearly eleven, when the doorbell rang. Not that it mattered, he was up, anyway, having given up on sleep once more, despite his lack of it the night before.

Ethan had spent that night admitting he'd blown it. He'd gotten angry when he shouldn't have. But he'd been so sure it was his inability to face the reality that lay behind the doors of The Oaks that had stood between them. He'd never realized that Layla had been holding back because she didn't believe him, that the whole time they'd been together she'd been waiting for it to end, waiting for him to decide he wanted the supermodel of the week and walk away from her.

It wasn't Layla's fault that she couldn't believe; it was his, for not giving her enough time. It was the damn world's fault, for convincing a beautiful, loving, generous, remarkable woman that she was somehow worth less because of her size.

He smothered the leap of hope his heart took at the door-bell, put down the book he'd been holding in an effort to pretend he'd been reading, and walked to the front door on bare feet. It was a hot summer night, and when he'd rolled out of bed he'd dressed only in sweatpants so he could leave a window open for some fresh air.

It must be Sarah, he thought. She was the only one who would show up this late and think nothing of it. He flipped on the porch light, then pulled the door open, forced words of teasing on his lips.

The words died unspoken.

In the golden glow of the light was an incredible sight.

A woman, tall, straight, bold, swathed in a cobalt-blue cape, her hair streaming down over her shoulders in a gleam-ing golden mass, her green eyes glowing turquoise even in the porch light. Her head was held determinedly high, and she met his startled gaze head-on.

"Hello, Ethan."

Her voice was low, husky, and he detected just the slightest note of edginess in it. As if she were uncertain of her welcome.

The shock of seeing her faded.

The realization of why she was there, in the gift he'd given her, the gift that had made her so nervous, struck. And in that moment he understood everything she was trying to say by wearing it.

"Layla," he breathed.

"I'm sorry," she began, but stopped when he shook his head.

He didn't need the words, it was all right there in her face, in her eyes. He could see forever in those eyes.

He held up his arms. She stepped into them. Instantly. He enveloped her in an embrace that would have cowed a lesser woman. Layla merely hugged him back, fiercely. For a long, silent, sweet moment he simply held her.

Then he pulled her into the house and shut the door behind her.

"Ethan, I—"

"Later," he said as he led her into the living room. "We can talk about it, all of it, later."

She fell silent. For a moment he just looked at her. Then, slowly, he lifted his hands to the fastening of the cape. "I love that you wore it. I know why you wore it. I want to see you wear it again, with me, so the whole world can see who you really are. But right now, I just want it *off.*"

Layla let out a long breath that he could tell held more than a tinge of relief. She let him unfasten the cape. It slipped off her shoulders into a vibrant blue pool at her feet. Venus rising from the water, he thought as she stood there in a silky slip of a dress he'd never seen before, a dress he would never have pictured her buying for herself. It flowed over her, not hiding her size but not hiding her shape, either, making clear the lovely proportions, emphasizing the richness of her curves and at the same time the fitness of her body.

She took his breath away, this luxurious woman.

And he couldn't wait to take hers away.

She reached for him then. Her fingers brushed over his naked chest, and he felt the muscles of his stomach clench.

It seemed like weeks, not merely hours, since he'd held her, touched her, felt her hands on him. When her hands slid beneath the waistband of his sweats, he inched closer, inviting her to explore farther. She did, her hands slipping down until she was cupping his buttocks, pulling him against her.

His body surged in response, urgently, eagerly. He nudged her with his hips, knowing she would feel, through the thin silk of that dress, how quickly she had aroused him.

"Still want to talk?" he asked thickly.

"Later," she agreed. "Much later."

She stepped back then. Her face was flushed, her breathing quickened, and he could see her taut, hardened nipples peaking the fabric over them.

"Forget the bedroom," he muttered. "I'll never make it."

The words seemed to fire them both, and in moments they were tugging at each other's clothing, shedding what little was left. Urgent, compelling need swamped them, and they went down to the floor, mouths locked together. Ethan shoved a table out of the way, heedless of what was on it.

The kiss deepened as they touched each other with a hint of desperation, as if they needed to be assured nothing had changed, that this coming together of theirs was as hot and furious as always. Ethan rolled, pulling her on top of him. He felt an instant of hesitation in Layla, knew what it was; they'd never made love in the light, and she'd never let him urge her on top before. He thought he knew why now, that she hadn't wanted him to see her clearly.

And then she moved, straddling him, agreeing to the change with an eagerness that told him more than he guessed she realized about her acceptance of everything he'd told her.

It was his last coherent thought. She eased herself down, taking him in with a searing, aching slowness that drove him to the edge of madness. And then, surer now, she began to ride him, driving him so deeply inside her that he thought he just might die of the pleasure. He bucked beneath her, and she responded, until the rhythm they set was fast, hard and wild. There was no holding back, not this time; he could feel it in her, could feel the full, uncontrolled passion of her for the first time.

It was hot, it was savage, it was explosive. And when it was done, when they both lay in exhausted repletion in each other's arms, they knew there was no hurry to say to each other in words what their bodies had just told them.

Epilogue

"**G**oing, going…gone! Sold, to our hosts, Ethan and Layla Winslow!"

The applause was louder than usual, and lasted longer, until it was obvious it was more for the buyers than the sale.

"I think it's going to look great over the fireplace of our new house," Ethan said to his wife, taking a last look at the painting—a sailboat heeled over in a fresh breeze—as it was carried away. They'd decided to start new, selling both their places and pooling the money to buy one of their own, together.

"Yes," she agreed. "It'll do nicely until we can get the real thing."

They were agreed on that, as well, that a sailboat was the perfect prescription to keep them both from terminal workaholism.

The applause continued, until the emcee—a kinder, gentler one Layla had handpicked this time—insisted they stand and take a bow.

It had been Layla's idea that the auction this year be of art and collectibles rather than people. And she had turned her considerable persuasive talents on many of Ethan's business associates and gotten some exciting donations. Ethan had gotten the feedback, which, to his amusement, had ranged from envy to rueful acknowledgment of her expertise in gentle but irresistible strong-arming.

They still got the occasional sideways glance as someone tried to figure them out, but it no longer bothered Layla. In fact, she usually returned the glance with a smile if it was innocent or regal disdain if it was more malicious. In either case, her point was made.

He loved her, passionately, deeply, and more than he'd ever thought he would love any woman.

And thankfully, now, she knew it. And returned it tenfold, giving him so much more. She was part of him now, and he didn't know how he'd managed without her for so long. She was there to share the joy, such as the day when, for a brief moment, Pete had recognized him, and the sorrow, as on the day when he'd learned there had been a setback on the Collins project. She'd helped him celebrate the first, and helped him regain his determination to succeed on the second. And his life had never been so complete.

They set a new record for the auction. They'd nearly equaled the center's budget for the year. The donation to The Oaks would be very healthy this year.

But as they went back to the brand-new home they'd just moved to yesterday—and where the only thing already set up was the bed—both Ethan and Layla knew there would never again be another auction as special as the one that had brought them together.

They both knew they'd gotten the best deal of all.

*   *   *   *   *

Author's Note

Breakthroughs in the study of Alzheimer's are being made every day, but the battle is still far from won. If you are lucky enough to live a life untouched by this devastating disease, please think of those who are not so fortunate. Contact your local, national or on-line Alzheimer's experts to see what you can do to help fight this ruthless thief.

Remember, for those who cannot.

If you enjoyed what you just read,
then we've got an offer you can't resist!

Take 2 bestselling
love stories FREE!

Plus get a FREE surprise gift!

Look Who's Celebrating Our 20th Anniversary:

Celebrate
20 YEARS

"Silhouette Desire is the purest form of contemporary romance."
—*New York Times* bestselling author
Elizabeth Lowell

"Let's raise a glass to Silhouette and all the great books and talented authors they've introduced over the past twenty years. May the *next* twenty be just as exciting and just as innovative!"
—*New York Times* bestselling author
Linda Lael Miller

"You've given us a sounding board, a place where, as readers, we can be entertained, and as writers, an opportunity to share our stories.... You deserve a special round of applause on...your twentieth birthday. Here's wishing you many, many more."
—International bestselling author
Annette Broadrick

Silhouette
Desire

SILHOUETTE'S 20ᵀᴴ ANNIVERSARY CONTEST
OFFICIAL RULES
NO PURCHASE NECESSARY TO ENTER

1. To enter, follow directions published in the offer to which you are responding. Contest begins 1/1/00 and ends on 8/24/00 (the "Promotion Period"). Method of entry may vary. Mailed entries must be postmarked by 8/24/00, and received by 8/31/00.

2. During the Promotion Period, the Contest may be presented via the Internet. Entry via the Internet may be restricted to residents of certain geographic areas that are disclosed on the Web site. To enter via the Internet, if you are a resident of a geographic area in which Internet entry is permissible, follow the directions displayed on-line, including typing your essay of 100 words or fewer telling us "Where In The World Your Love Will Come Alive." On-line entries must be received by 11:59 p.m. Eastern Standard time on 8/24/00. Limit one e-mail entry per person, household and e-mail address per day, per presentation. If you are a resident of a geographic area in which entry via the Internet is permissible, you may, in lieu of submitting an entry on-line, enter by mail, by hand-printing your name, address, telephone number and contest number/name on an 8"x 11" plain piece of paper and telling us in 100 words or fewer "Where In The World Your Love Will Come Alive," and mailing via first-class mail to: Silhouette 20ᵗʰ Anniversary Contest, (in the U.S.) P.O. Box 9069, Buffalo, NY 14269-9069; (In Canada) P.O. Box 637, Fort Erie, Ontario, Canada L2A 5X3. Limit one 8"x 11" mailed entry per person, household and e-mail address per day. On-line and/or 8"x 11" mailed entries received from persons residing in geographic areas in which Internet entry is not permissible will be disqualified. No liability is assumed for lost, late, incomplete, inaccurate, nondelivered or misdirected mail, or misdirected e-mail, for technical, hardware or software failures of any kind, lost or unavailable network connection, or failed, incomplete, garbled or delayed computer transmission or any human error which may occur in the receipt or processing of the entries in the contest.

3. Essays will be judged by a panel of members of the Silhouette editorial and marketing staff based on the following criteria:

> Sincerity (believability, credibility)—50%
>
> Originality (freshness, creativity)—30%
>
> Aptness (appropriateness to contest ideas)—20%

Purchase or acceptance of a product offer does not improve your chances of winning. In the event of a tie, duplicate prizes will be awarded.

4. All entries become the property of Harlequin Enterprises Ltd., and will not be returned. Winner will be determined no later than 10/31/00 and will be notified by mail. Grand Prize winner will be required to sign and return Affidavit of Eligibility within 15 days of receipt of notification. Noncompliance within the time period may result in disqualification and an alternative winner may be selected. All municipal, provincial, federal, state and local laws and regulations apply. Contest open only to residents of the U.S. and Canada who are 18 years of age or older, and is void wherever prohibited by law. Internet entry is restricted solely to residents of those geographical areas in which Internet entry is permissible. Employees of Torstar Corp., their affiliates, agents and members of their immediate families are not eligible. Taxes on the prizes are the sole responsibility of winners. Entry and acceptance of any prize offered constitutes permission to use winner's name, photograph or other likeness for the purposes of advertising, trade and promotion on behalf of Torstar Corp. without further compensation to the winner, unless prohibited by law. Torstar Corp and D.L. Blair, Inc., their parents, affiliates and subsidiaries, are not responsible for errors in printing or electronic presentation of contest or entries. In the event of printing or other errors which may result in unintended prize values or duplication of prizes, all affected contest materials or entries shall be null and void. If for any reason the Internet portion of the contest is not capable of running as planned, including infection by computer virus, bugs, tampering, unauthorized intervention, fraud, technical failures, or any other causes beyond the control of Torstar Corp. which corrupt or affect the administration, secrecy, fairness, integrity or proper conduct of the contest, Torstar Corp. reserves the right, at its sole discretion, to disqualify any individual who tampers with the entry process and to cancel, terminate, modify or suspend the contest or the Internet portion thereof. In the event of a dispute regarding an on-line entry, the entry will be deemed submitted by the authorized holder of the e-mail account submitted at the time of entry. Authorized account holder is defined as the natural person who is assigned to an e-mail address by an Internet access provider, on-line service provider or other organization that is responsible for arranging e-mail address for the domain associated with the submitted e-mail address.

5. Prizes: Grand Prize—a $10,000 vacation to anywhere in the world. Travelers (at least one must be 18 years of age or older) or parent or guardian if one traveler is a minor, must sign and return a Release of Liability prior to departure. Travel must be completed by December 31, 2001, and is subject to space and accommodations availability. Two hundred (200) Second Prizes—a two-book limited edition autographed collector set from one of the Silhouette Anniversary authors: Nora Roberts, Diana Palmer, Linda Howard or Annette Broadrick (value $10.00 each set). All prizes are valued in U.S. dollars.

6. For a list of winners (available after 10/31/00), send a self-addressed, stamped envelope to: Harlequin Silhouette 20ᵗʰ Anniversary Winners, P.O. Box 4200, Blair, NE 68009-4200.

Contest sponsored by Torstar Corp., P.O. Box 9042, Buffalo, NY 14269-9042.

ENTER FOR A CHANCE TO WIN*

Silhouette's 20th Anniversary Contest

Tell Us Where in the World You Would Like *Your* Love To Come Alive... And We'll Send the Lucky Winner There!

Silhouette wants to take you wherever your happy ending can come true.

Here's how to enter: Tell us, in 100 words or less, where you want to go to make your love come alive!

In addition to the grand prize, there will be 200 runner-up prizes, collector's-edition book sets autographed by one of the Silhouette anniversary authors: **Nora Roberts, Diana Palmer, Linda Howard** or **Annette Broadrick**.

DON'T MISS YOUR CHANCE TO WIN! ENTER NOW! No Purchase Necessary

Silhouette®
Where love comes alive™

Name: _____

Address: _____

City: _____ State/Province: _____

Zip/Postal Code: _____

Mail to Harlequin Books: **In the U.S.:** P.O. Box 9069, Buffalo, NY 14269-9069; **In Canada:** P.O. Box 637, Fort Erie, Ontario, L4A 5X3

*No purchase necessary—for contest details send a self-addressed stamped envelope to: Silhouette's 20th Anniversary Contest, P.O. Box 9069, Buffalo, NY, 14269-9069 (include contest name on self-addressed envelope). Residents of Washington and Vermont may omit postage. Open to Cdn. (excluding Quebec) and U.S. residents who are 18 or over. Void where prohibited. Contest ends August 31, 2000.

PS20CON_R